Chico and Dan

by Harold Keith

Illustrations by Scott Arbuckle

EAKIN PRESS ★ Austin, Texas

Published in the United States of America
By Eakin Press
A Division of Sunbelt Media, Inc.
P.O. Box 90159
Austin, Texas 78709
Email: eakinpub@sig.net

2 3 4 5 6 7 8 9

ISBN 1-57168-216-3

Contents

To my son
Johnny Keith
and my
Texas and New Mexico great-grandchildren
Virginia and Kenneth Hollinger
and Sarai, Ysaac, Casey Rose, and Amanda Keith

Author's Note

To find out about wild horses in the West and Southwest, I tracked them in libraries and museums in Santa Fe, Albuquerque, Taos, Phoenix, Sedona, Carson City, and Alamosa. I also researched them heavily in the University of Oklahoma Library and its excellent Western History Collection. I am grateful to them all.

However, I owe the most to a personal source I consulted. He was the late Les Headlee, a retired eighty-six-year-old rancher living in Alamosa, Colorado. Mr. Headlee's last ranch, the Cross Arrow, was located in Conejos County, Colorado, at the confluence of the Conejos River and the Rio Grande.

Of wild horses, Mr. Headlee said, "Some of the best horses I ever owned were wild ones I had broken. They had a great sense of smell. They knew where they were going and what they were doing. They could turn a cow quicker than any I ever saw. A saddle fit them better. They had a smoother gait. You could put fifty miles on them in a day. They were affectionate and loyal."

I visited him on three different occasions before his death. I am very appreciative of his help. I should also like to thank the lady who first put me in touch with him, Christine E. Moeny, a librarian at Adams State College in Alamosa, Colorado.

I am thankful to Mrs. Addie Lee Barker, my former associate at the University of Oklahoma, for typing and editing; it has meant much to the project.

Also, I am grateful to the late Mrs. Mary Esther Saxon, former assistant professor of bibliography at the University of Oklahoma, for having provided the faculty study in which I researched and wrote much of this book.

HAROLD KEITH
Sports Publicity Director Emeritus
The University of Oklahoma
Norman, Oklahoma

The Runaway

The boy came out of the Nevada heat into the sitting room of the ranch house, chewing on a twig as he bore the dull ache in his heart.

Across the room, the old man sat sternly in a rocking chair and looked him over, up and down. The old man's legs were so bowed that he seemed to sit around the chair instead of in it. Despite the ninety-degree heat outside, he had a little fire going in the big stone fireplace.

"What's yer name, boy?" he snapped in a peevish, high-pitched voice. His shiny dome was ringed with a ruff of white hair. His beard covered his face, almost to his eyes.

"Dan Deweese, sir," the boy replied.

"How old are you?"

"Eleven, sir."

Hitching up his pants, the boy stood there, a lonely, pathetic figure, hungry for kindness. His hands clutched his old, tan hat. His gray eyes peered out fearlessly from behind bushy brows that almost met.

"How'd you git here?" the old man demanded. It was a logical question. The only railroad that crossed

the state lay forty miles distant. It was almost a day's
ride between ranches.

"Walked a lot of the way, sir," said the boy.
"Caught some rides."

"Why'd you come here?" the old man asked,
thrusting his whiskery face closer. His words lashed
out accusingly.

For a moment the boy stared at him defiantly.
How could this grouchy old fellow know that the
dream of his life was to have a horse of his own? A
horse to feed, and brush, and ride, and love? How
could he know the hurt of somebody who had just
had all this, and lost it?

"Because you're Buck Boyce, my great-uncle,
and I had no place else to go," the boy answered. He
enjoyed the look of surprise on the old man's face.

"My mother sent me," he added. "She's Gladys
Deweese. Her father was your brother, John. She
thought you might give me a job."

"Humpf!" growled the old man. "Why'd she send
you way out here on me? Couldn't you git along with
your own mother?"

2

With one hand, the boy reached up and nervously twisted his shirt collar. *He's just like Ma warned me he'd be*, he told himself, *about as friendly as that hickory whiffletree on the Costenaga wagon I saw outside.*

"Sir, it wasn't my mother I couldn't get along with," said the boy. He was reluctant to air his troubles to a stranger.

"Then who was it?" snarled the old man, his voice rising irritably. "Speak up, boy. It couldn't have been yore father. He's been dead six or seven years."

For a moment the boy looked at him stubbornly and was on the verge of refusing to reveal what was tormenting him. But his feet were sore and the calves of his legs throbbed. He said to himself, *no use trying to hide anything. Just as well tell him and get it over with. Or he might not let me stay.*

"It's my stepdad, sir," he said. "I hate to unload my troubles on you, but I will if you want me to. Last year, I saved up ten dollars doing chores for a neighbor. When I told my stepdad I was going to buy a box of carpenter tools with it, he shook his head and advised me to give it to him for safe keeping. I did. Then I was taken sick with typhoid fever. When I got well I asked him for my money but he said he had paid it all out for medicine while I was sick."

At the galling thought of it, the boy planted his feet angrily and felt his toes squirming in his old shoes.

"Another time," he went on, "I earned six dollars and bought nine hens and a rooster. Soon I was selling eggs and friers. At the end of the year I had almost fifteen dollars. One day when I was at school my stepdad ran across my little nest egg I had hidden in a closet. He took it. He deposited it in the bank under his own name. When I asked him for it, he gave me three dollars, saying that he had to charge me for the chicken feed."

3

He fell silent for a moment, wringing his hands and wetting his lips with his tongue. All that could be heard was the lick of the flames in the fireplace.

"Worst of all was about my mare," he resumed, his voice quieter now. "Last winter I did chores for my cousin. Last month, he paid me twenty-five dollars for my work, two ten-dollar gold pieces and a five-dollar bill. I bought me a mare and a saddle. I liked the mare a lot. She was all mine. Sometimes I'd mount her at nine in the morning and wouldn't get off her until five in the evening.

"One day when I was gone to school, my stepfather sold my mare to a cattle buyer coming through. He was mad because I hadn't consulted him. He told me he had deposited the money in the bank at three percent interest and that he would give it to me later to go to college on. We quarreled about it. He started to whip me so I ran off. I couldn't stand him anymore."

"Humpf!" the old man hooted. "Do you always run off when you can't stand somethin'?"

The boy looked at him in astonishment. He drew another long breath and blew it out. He felt his throat knotting. *Well*, he mused, *I can't take this kind of talk*

much longer. Looks like I'll soon be back out there, hoofing it on that road again with only the sage and the rabbit brush to keep me company.

"What kind of work kin you do?" Buck Boyce asked suddenly.

The boy's chin lifted in surprise. "I can ride, an' rope, an' herd cattle, an' fork hay," he said.

Old Buck grunted scornfully. "Can you milk?"

Dan Deweese flinched and knew that the old man saw it. No boy working on a ranch liked to milk.

"Yessir," he admitted. Actually, he had done most of the family milking back home.

A tall man whose straight red hair was parted in the middle and carefully combed to either side came in, smiling pleasantly. The cleft in his chin was so deep that Dan believed that he could have stuck a raisin in it, except he felt too tired to lift the raisin even if he'd had one.

Using his arms as levers, old Buck pushed himself up from the rocker to his feet. Dan Deweese saw that the interview was over.

"You kin sleep in the bunkhouse with the hands," he said curtly. "We'll try you out." Turning, he began to shuffle papers in an open desk.

Dan Deweese stiffened and his mouth fell apart with surprise. He felt shamed and ill at ease. Although the ranch house looked big and well furnished, a blood relationship apparently meant very little to old Buck Boyce. But Dan was glad to have any kind of shelter.

The old man turned to the red-haired man. "This here boy is my great-nephew," he said. "He wants a job. Find him somethin' to do."

The old man began staring at something out the window, something that seemed to disturb him greatly. "Ranged cow's in the garden agin," he muttered. "I'm gonna have to git out in this heat, saddle a hoss an' run her out."

5

Reaching for his hat, he headed for the door. He paid no heed to Dan, nor the red-haired man, but brushed right past them.

The red-haired man laughed easily. "That's just like an old-time cowman," he said, shaking his head. "It's a hundred yards to the barn, and only forty to the cow, but Mr. Boyce has got to ride."

He looked at Dan, as if seeing him for the first time. Dan knew what he saw—a boy who was all skin and bones and dirt. And one who was very tired and hungry.

"I'm Ben Dragoo," the red-haired man said. "I'll take you to Tonia," he added. "She's Mr. Boyce's cook and housekeeper."

"Is there a Mrs. Boyce?" Dan wanted to know.

"Used to be," Ben replied. "But she died some years back."

Ben and Dan found Tonia outdoors, a black shawl around her head and shoulders. She had been washing. Wet garments were spread on the sage bushes that grew everywhere. Every branch blossomed with shirts, blouses, trousers, and socks colored as gaily as a peacock's feathers—orange, green, gypsy red, and dandelion yellow.

Ben Dragoo introduced them. "This is Dan Deweese, Mr. Boyce's great-nephew," he said. "He needs a bath, clean clothes, and a chair close to the action at the supper table tonight. He's stayin' in the bunkhouse."

José, Tonia's husband, was a cowboy, Ben Dragoo had told Dan. He did most of the outfit's roping. Carmen, Tonia's cousin, did most of the cooking for the cowhands in the cook house.

With one quick sympathetic look, Tonia took in Dan's situation. "Sí, sí, Mr. Dragoo," she spoke in musical syllables. Ben Dragoo strode off to the barns.

To Dan, she said, "Nevada's the driest state in the Union in rainfall, señor, but we've got a pump and a good well here." She pointed to a small well house nearby. "It's got a tub in it. I'll get you some soap and clean clothing, and while you bathe I'll wash the things you are wearing."

"Thank you, ma'am," said Dan.

Her hospitality lifted his spirits.

"Who's Mr. Dragoo?" he asked. Wide-eyed, she stared at him, as if everybody should know who Ben Dragoo was.

"He's Mr. Boyce's foreman," she said. She looked again at Dan's ragged attire. An expression of sadness came upon her brown face.

"We have plenty of clothing for a *muchacho* like you," she said. "Nevada's not only the driest state in the Union, but it also has the fewest women and children. Right now, there isn't another boy living within fifty miles of here. But there was—once—and he was about your size."

Wet lashes hid her black eyes and her voice became hushed.

"He was Chico, our son," she said. "A bronc fell on him."

"Ma'am, I'm truly sorry," said Dan. He pitied her profoundly.

She sniffed once and recovered herself. "We still have his clothing and no one to give it to—til you came. Wait *uno momento* and I'll get it for you."

After Dan bathed, dressed, and combed his hair, the foreman took him to the bunkhouse of cottonwood logs. He assigned him a bed in a corner. Bridles, saddles, and ropes hung from the walls. The odor of unwashed men, sweaty boots, dry cow manure, and smoke from the coal-oil lamps was everywhere. On the wooden floor various articles of clothing were thrown in wild disorder.

But the walls were whitewashed. A cleansing breeze blew from the roofed hall, or breezeway, to a combination mess hall and cook house that was attached.

"It's kinda whiffy in here," apologized Ben Dragoo.

7

"The boys hang their clothes on the floor so they won't fall down and get lost. But they're a good bunch. Mr. Boyce and me sorted 'em out pretty careful."

After supper, Dan went early to bed. The buckaroos, as Ben Dragoo called the cow hands, came in later but Dan never heard them.

It seemed he had hardly closed his eyes when he felt a hand shaking his shoulder. A delightful smell of something he guessed was ham and eggs came from the cook house. He heard the lowing of cows being driven in for milking, and the splash and clinking of buckets at the well.

Dan jumped right up and dressed. He felt wonderfully refreshed. He hurried to the shed to help with the milking. José, Tonia's husband, shot one long melancholy look at the pants and shirt Dan wore, then wordlessly handed him a bucket. He pointed to a black cow feeding from a box in a nearby stall.

Dan went right to work.

The Wild Foal

fter breakfast, while Dan was at the woodpile chopping up juniper and pine, a force came into his life that was to change its entire direction.

A wild colt, a wobbly little fellow only a few hours old, wandered into the pony pasture with the remuda, as the ranch's extra saddle horses were called.

The orphan was a grulla of delicate smallness. A black stripe ran down his back and legs from his shoulders to his knees. His legs were so long that he looked absurdly like a horse on stilts.

Dan gawked at him with wonder and awe. Dropping his axe, the boy joined the ranch hands clustered around him. He was sorely tempted to pick him up in his arms. The foal's shoulders stood only a little higher than Dan's hips.

The colt was soon surrounded by the saddle horses. It seemed to Dan that they were trying to show affection to him, protect him, and contend among themselves for outright possession of him.

An old buckskin fought off all the others and began trying to play with him, biting him gently along the flank, then shying back and running off a few steps as if inviting him to romp.

"Look at that old fool!" said one of the cowhands.

"Everybody loves a baby," said another.

But the tiny orphan was too weak to play. Bewildered, he moved from one saddle horse to another searching for the one he wanted. But she wasn't there.

"A mockey will seldom go back after her colt that has been left behind in a wild flight," said George Claxton, a lean muscled cowpuncher with jet black hair. "This one probably found our saddle horses in the night."

Dan could hardly believe his ears. It seemed incredible to him that any mother would desert her offspring, especially one as small and lonely looking as this one.

Old Buck shambled up from the blacksmith shop. Although the day was growing warmer, he was wearing an old red sweater of soft wool. Despite its shabby appearance, it was obviously a favorite of his.

The old man wiped a gnat off his neck and squinted at the homeless waif. Too small to graze, it could only lap helplessly at the water puddled beside the tank. The old man was scowling.

"Jest as well put a slug 'tween his eyes," he barked. "He's starvin' to death."

Dan cringed. He hated to see any animal shot for any reason.

Lee Rawson, a young buster with a blond mustache, took a deep drag on his cigarette and was seized by a coughing fit.

"Aw cripes, I'll do it," he growled. "Loan me a gun, somebody. My pistol's packed away in my bedroll."

"No!" burst out Dan, dismayed at the harsh suggestion. He stared open-mouthed at Rawson and then at his great-uncle. His heart was hammering. The others stared at him, surprised by his boldness.

Dan stepped forward, confronting the old man. His eyes were big with anxious longing.

"Give him to me, Uncle Buck," he blurted

10

eagerly. "I'll raise him. I'll take keer of him." He couldn't understand why he was the only one who wanted to save the colt. They should all be trying to save him, it seemed to Dan.

The old man glared at him. "A young colt keeps runnin' to its mammy ever few minutes to refresh itself," he said. "It can't live without its mammy's fresh warm milk. Who's this 'un gonna run to when it gits hongry?"

"It can run to me," said Dan eagerly. "I'll give it cow's milk."

Old Buck snorted. "Cow's milk!" he growled scornfully. "A colt born jest last night can digest only the milk it gits from its mammy. A mare's milk is the richest on the range. Anyhow—how you gonna git cow's milk down its throat?"

Tonia, who with Carmen had joined the group to see the new arrival, became a surprise participant in the discussion.

"There is a way, *señor* Boyce," she said, pleasantly. "We used it once to save a baby lamb whose mother was killed by a wolf back on the San Saba. It was lots of trouble, but it can be done if gone about in the right way."

Dan pushed his old hat back on his head and felt thrilled to his toes. Trouble? Who cared about trouble when a life as cute and precious as this one was at stake?

Surprised, old Buck glared at her.

Tonia's kindly voice purred on. "We used a bottle and a rubber nipple to feed the little lamb. We were careful to feed it from a cow that did not give rich milk. We added to each pint of milk a spoonful of sugar and a little water. At first, we fed it eight times each day, a half pint to each feeding. You have to use milk from the same cow. It has to be freshly drawn each time.

"When the little one was four weeks old, we taught it to drink skim milk from a pail," she concluded, "but that's something that takes a long time to learn."

"I'll milk the cow," Dan volunteered. "I'll feed him."

Tonia shot a timid sideways glance at Uncle Buck and then her gaze came back to Dan. She said, "If you'll do that, *señor* Dan, I'll prepare the bottles and the nipples each day. I'll scald them and keep them clean."

Old Buck threw up his hands and headed for the house.

"It ain't gonna make no difference what any of you do," he sputtered over his shoulder. "He ain't gonna live no how."

At first, it looked as if he was right. Tonia came out with a nipple and a bottle. The bottle was filled with milk Dan had taken a minute earlier from the black cow. Tonia had diluted it with warm water and added sugar.

But the mouse-colored baby would have nothing to do with the strange mixture. When they tried gently to force the rubber nipple into his mouth, he jerked his head up and spat milk all over them, sniffing and coughing and snorting to get it out of his nose.

As the morning waned, the little one grew tired and weary. Jaded from his long walk behind the remuda the night before, and famished for food, he stood swaying on his long, pipestem legs. Dan's eyes filmed over. He could hardly bear it. The colt was dying on its feet.

Just the thought of that ruined Dan's own meal. Although Carmen had prepared Mexican sausage, baked eggs, refried beans, and hot corn bread, Dan couldn't eat. In the middle of the meal he left the table to go to the corral and stay with the wild colt.

But when the boy came close, the foal caught his scent and shied away, his long ears slanting backward.

Dan thought, *no wonder he won't take up with me. He's as wild as the coyotes, the wolves and the antelope that roam these sagebrush plains, and the mountains dense with piñon beyond them. I'm the first human being he's ever seen up close, or heard, or smelled, or felt the touch of. It's all very strange to him.*

Late in the afternoon, Ben Dragoo rode in from the range on his bay horse with a black mane and tail. He got off at the well. Leading his mount, he came up and took a long careful look at the helpless infant. Then he turned appealingly to Dan.

"It'd be a kindness to him, young man, if you'd let me put him on my horse and take him out on the prairie," he said gently. "I'd carry him in my arms across my saddle. I'd take him so far that you couldn't hear my gun. I'd bury him so deep that the coyotes could never dig him up."

Dan's throat tightened. He bit down on his trembling lip. Doggedly, he shook his head.

Just before supper, Carmen came out with the freshly scrubbed milk pail, bottle, and nipple.

"Tonia says to try one more time," she said, handing the bucket to Dan. Dan went to the cow which he kept in the barn. He milked the bucket a third full. Tonia came out of the kitchen. She filled the bottle with the bubbly milk. She added the sugar and the water. She attached the rubber nipple.

But the baby refused to drink. He wanted his mother. He wanted his real dinner. He didn't want sympathy or petting. And Dan, wretched from disappointment and grief, gave up. He backed off, hot tears prickling his eyes.

And then the tiny visitor did an astonishing, unbelievable thing. Suddenly, he stuck his nose in

Dan's milk pail and drank as if he'd been doing it all his life!

When they tried to take the bucket away to prevent him from foundering, he fought weakly to keep his mouth in the warm overflow. His short tail switching vigorously, he swallowed in strangled gulps.

"Look at him go for it!" Dan shouted. Laughing joyously, he thought with satisfaction that no matter what lay ahead, a colt as spunky as this one surely had a chance.

First Lessons

At first, it seemed only a slender chance. Constipation, that enemy of all horses, young or old, set in. Dan began worrying again.

Tonia was equal to the challenge. She ordered the first ration fed the colt each morning sweetened with molasses. The crisis passed.

When scouring occurred, Ben Dragoo offered the correct remedy. "Put a little scorched flour and lime water into the milk," he suggested to Tonia and Carmen. They did. The patient slowly began to improve.

But until he did, Dan worried himself sick. "I worry about everything," he told Ben. "I worry that I haven't got him cooled down good when I take him out. I worry about him comin' down with a cold."

"You gotta watch him careful," said Ben. "He's an early bloomin' colt. They get crippled easy, or somethin' happens to 'em. This one's awful skinny because his mother ain't here to feed him."

Dan liked staying in the bunkhouse now. It put him nearer the colt. It made the night feedings easier and faster.

Feeding problems were not all that troubled the foundling. Although Dan kept the youngster's stall dry and clean and filled with fresh straw, it wandered around restlessly. It could not be induced to lie down.

Dan grew so desperate that he was ready to try anything. On the seventh night, he went into the colt's stall. He spread a couple of horse blankets over the straw. Kicking off his shoes, he lay down. In the tenderest tones he could muster, he called the colt to him.

"Let's take a nap," he proposed.

For a moment, the little grulla cocked his ears. He nosed Dan all over, giving him a couple of bunts in the ribs. Like a big dog, he took a couple of turns around the stall.

Then his long legs bent and he flopped down beside Dan. He snuggled as closely to the boy as possible. He seemed to be saying, "This was all I wanted—just a little sympathy and companionship." And Dan felt so happy that he almost shouted with joy.

After that, he no longer worried about whether the orphan would live. His greatest fear now was that somebody else might try to take it from him.

It soon became evident that nobody else wanted the new arrival. Horses were plentiful on the Bar-B. Everybody seemed busy with his own string.

Although Dan was busy chopping wood, picking apples, and milking twice daily, he found time to go to the corral and handle the baby all over. Pushing and pulling it gently about, he strove to fix the habit of obedience in it.

"Nobody should feed and handle him but you," Ben Dragoo advised. "And you should do it every day. I know I don't have to tell you to handle him gently, without scarin' him."

"Yessir," said Dan, gratefully.

Dan was always careful to speak to the wild colt in a friendly manner. He knew that tone of voice is a universal language and every living animal understands it. He could not have scolded him anyhow, so deep was his affection for him.

16

On the morning the colt was three weeks old, Ben Dragoo brought Dan a small halter of soft leather he had fashioned in the blacksmith shop.

"I think this'll fit him snug around the nose and under the throat" said the foreman. "We don't want him to catch a foot in it, do we?"

Dan shook his head vigorously. "No sir!" he said positively. "Sure don't."

Later, Dan walked up to the little animal. He patted the colt on the back and shoulder. He held out his hand to be licked. With lots of petting and baby talk, he slowly slipped the strap around its neck. Then the head went through the halter without the least show of resistance.

Twice a day, Dan slid the halter on the colt and led him about gently but firmly, a step or two at a time. In the quietest manner possible, he then removed the halter, stroking the colt's head and neck so it would know that he was still its friend.

Soon the wild colt became so accustomed to the halter that he could be led about and even tied up for short periods.

Dan was delighted. "He catches on to everything real quick," he told Ben.

Affection was the key. "I try to make him know how much I like him," Dan told Tonia one morning when she brought the clean milk pail. "I think he likes me, too."

He looked at her shyly. "If you and José don't mind, I'd like to name him Chico, after your son," he said. He hoped she'd be pleased. In his view, it was the finest compliment he could bestow.

A low moan, heavy with sorrow and tender feelings, escaped Tonia. "Oh!" she breathed, her soft voice barely audible, "Oh . . ."

Dan, watching her keenly, misunderstood her emotion. "Ma'am, if you'd rather I didn't, I'll be glad to call him something else," he said.

"Oh no, *señor* Dan," she murmured, "you honor us with your kindness." Tears swam in her eyes as loving memories engulfed her.

Dan was pleased. He blinked, wetting his lips with his tongue. "He wouldn't be alive today if it hadn't been for you," he told her.

Later, Ben and Dan were discussing Tonia. "She's the greatest," Ben told the boy. "She's a good house-keeper. She's loyal, cheerful, clean, and never complains. She's a good cook. She takes fine care of Mr. Boyce and his house."

Every morning, Dan would take Chico to the pony pasture and watch him run. The youngster loved to run. He flew over the buffalo grass, his stub tail twinkling. When only a few weeks old, a wild colt can scamper almost as fast as a grown mustang. A gallop is as natural a gait to it as a walk to a domestic animal.

Dan was thrilled by the colt's running style. Chico ran with long springy strides. The farther he reached out with his long legs, the nearer he got to the ground. It seemed to Dan that he skimmed the meadows so closely that his stomach almost brushed the pasture grass.

Once when the foal caught a virus that impaired his breathing, he still ran so hard that Dan had to go out into the pasture and quiet him. The anxious boy borrowed an old woven wire cot from Tonia and José. Spreading his blankets upon it, he slept for three nights in front of the colt's stall. The colt's throat got well.

Whenever Dan wished to call the orphan to him, he would go to the fence and whistle sharply. Instantly the colt's head would fly up and he would come on the run. He always came right up to Dan and began pushing against him with his nose.

All this exercise made the colt very hungry. As he grew older, the feedings were reduced to six times a day, and then to four. The new milk was gradually changed to skim milk. The quantity was slowly increased. Both the colt and his appetite grew.

Oats were introduced to the colt and became a part of his diet. "Oats is a horse's beef and potatoes," Ben told Dan as he showed him the granary where the oats were kept. Chico ate less oats than the other colts on the ranch, yet stayed in good condition. Like his wild relatives, he didn't need as much.

However, the corral feed box was too high for him to reach. Dan went to the lumber pile. Taking tools from the blacksmith shop, he began building a low feed box for his pet.

Then he remembered that the lumber wasn't his. Ben had gone to town with the supply wagon. Dan went to old Buck for permission.

"Uncle Buck," he began, "Chico's too small to reach the manger in the corral. He's started eatin' oats. Can I borrow some boards from the lumber pile and build him a low feed box he can reach?"

The old man looked as cross as a snapping turtle.

"Who said to start him on oats?" he demanded, gruffly.

"Ben," said Dan.

"Humpf!" growled the old man. "Why should I waste good grain on a miserable broomtail like him?"

Dan's heart sank. It sounded like his great-uncle was in his usual quarrelsome mood.

"You can take some of the wood from the big pile behind the blacksmith shop," said the old man, walking away.

Dan was thunderstruck. It was the first time his great-uncle had read him the riot act, then changed his mind.

"Thank you, sir," he said. But the old man had gone around the corner.

Occasionally, Dan would ask Carmen for lumps of sugar. Not only did Chico mouth them greedily, he learned to nose in Dan's shirt pocket searching for them.

Dan looked at him constantly and liked what he saw. The wild colt held his head up boldly. His eyes were large, lustrous and wide-set. His ears darted and flitted this way and that. He noticed everything going on around him, chasing the cloud shadows, snorting at the snapping grasshoppers, and listening to the chirping of the barn swallows.

When it became plain to everybody that the waif would live, old Buck finally conceded it. But he did it in a left-handed way.

"Humpf!" he grunted one night at the barn. "Only thing a wild broomtail is good fer is to keep the kids out of the house."

At first, Dan resented the remark. *It isn't Chico that keeps me out of the ranch house,* he thought. *It's you.* But as he downed his second glass of milk at supper, he felt a surge of triumph. *At least Uncle Buck acknowledges the colt's existence,* he told himself. *He's stopped saying that he's going to starve to death. He's stopped talking about shooting him.*

But the old man's true opinion surfaced a week later when he came to the barn with Ben Dragoo.

While they were standing under the corral shed talking, Chico came in quietly behind them. The colt started nudging in old Buck's pocket.

Startled, the old man whirled about. Snatching off his big hat, he struck the colt heavily across the face with it.

"Git away from me, you wild thing!" he yelled.

The orphan jumped back, bewildered and confused. It was the first blow he had ever suffered and the first cross word ever spoken to him. He shrank back against a nearby manger.

"Don't hit him, Uncle Buck," Dan protested, coming forward from the well where he had gone to get a drink. "He wasn't doin' nothin' to you. He was just huntin' in your pocket for a lump of sugar, like he does in mine. He was just tryin' to make friends."

The old man swung 'round on Dan, his face twisting with anger.

"I'll pick my own friends on this ranch," he retorted. "He'll never be nothin' but a no-good broomtail. I don't want no danged broomy slobberin' on me."

Dan went to the colt. Speaking to it kindly, he pushed it ahead of him out of the barn.

"Don't go 'round him anymore for anything," he told Chico, patting him gently on the shoulder and neck and speaking to him as if he was intelligent enough to understand. "All he's got in his pocket anyhow is his plug of chewin' tobacco. You wouldn't like that."

He cradled the colt's head in one arm, laying his cheek against its nose. He hoped that the incident had not alarmed Chico too greatly. He didn't want anything to break the colt's spirit.

"I'll get you some sugar tonight," he promised.

Dan walked back to the orchard, his forehead furrowed in thought. He wondered why his great-uncle hated Chico. He's the only horse on the ranch that he does hate, he told himself bitterly.

That night, while Dan was feeding the colt, he was still fretting about it. Ben Dragoo dropped by.

"You're lookin' awful gloomy tonight, young man," the foreman said. "What's the matter?"

Dan lowered the pail so that the orphan could drink. He said, "Uncle Buck called Chico a no-good broomtail. He don't think he'll ever amount to anything. He hates him."

Ben Dragoo shifted his hat to the back of his head. "Don't get down on your colt just because Mr. Boyce don't like him," he said. "He feels that way about all the wild ones. Some day I'll tell you why."

With one hand, he pointed toward Chico, who was drinking vigorously. "This one is gonna make a good cow horse if you handle him right."

Surprised, Dan looked at him, as if to say: "How do you know that?"

21

C.4

Ben said, "Some of the best cow horses I ever owned was the wild ones I captured and broke. They had a great sense of smell. They knew where they were goin' and what they were doin' every minute. They was fast and tough. They had a smooth gait. They didn't jolt you. The saddle fit 'em better because they wasn't sheep-backed like a lot of the domestic stock. They could turn a cow on a dime."

He wiped his hands on the sides of his pants. "They're smart and they've got good memories. You can put fifty miles on one of 'em in a day's time. But Mr. Boyce and lots of other ranchmen don't like 'em. So I never bring one on the place."

Ben's words were cheering. Dan's spirit lifted as he watched Chico slurp skimmed milk from the bucket. But he still wondered why his great-uncle disliked the wild ones so fervidly.

Why don't I ask him why? Dan thought. *I'm not afraid of him.*

Next morning, the boy took the question directly to old Buck himself.

The Abduction of Jewel

Old Buck was sitting in the blacksmith shop, searching through his tool chest for a washer. He was wearing his red sweater. He'd already had breakfast and a smoke, Dan knew. He looked halfway affable and civilized.

Boldly, Dan walked up to him.

"Uncle Buck, what have you got against wild horses?" he asked.

The old man spun around. Instantly his mood changed. He gave Dan his angry snapping turtle look.

"All right, I'll tell you what I got agin' em," he said fiercely. "They're the worst pests on the range. At the salt licks they fight my cattle away from the salt. At the water hole they break up the feed troughs runnin' back and forth while hundreds of my cattle wait to drink. When they see a man comin' on horseback, even if he's a mile away, they panic, tearin' through my herd, knockin' down cows and killin' calves. On the roundup, they stampede right through my cattle and it takes hours of hard ridin' to check the drift and get the cattle headed fer the roundup grounds agin."

There was a smolder in his eyes, a steady hate. He went on, "In early spring, when the ground is wet, they cut up the grass with their sharp hooves. In summer, they eat the range grass, clippin' it closer than a sheep. They drink the precious water of a country bad in need of it. They steal an' drive off some of my best saddle hosses and mares. Nobody dares turn the saddle hosses out in winter like we did in the old days."

Dan just stood and listened, shocked at the crimes laid to the wild ones. He hadn't dreamed that mustangs caused so much mischief. Now he was more mixed up than ever. Ben liked the wild ones. Uncle Buck hated them. Both sounded sincere. Who was he to believe?

That night, he hunted up Ben Dragoo at the little house where the foreman lived with his wife. Ben was sitting on the back step. With a knife, he was cleaning the mud off his boots. It was still hot. A bead of sweat ran out of the cleft in his chin.

Dan told him about asking Uncle Buck why he disliked wild horses, and what the old man had said.

Ben Dragoo stood, a boot in one hand. He turned his head and spat in the dust. For a moment he just looked at Dan, saying nothing. Then he spoke, quietly.

"Mr. Boyce didn't tell you the real reason," he said. "It's true that he don't like your hoss. But what you don't know is that he hates all wild hosses, or colts, or mares, or studs. Most of all he hates Gaunch, the brown stallion that's the boss of the wild bunch that lives 'round here and steals the mares on all the ranches."

Ben paused a moment to wipe the back of one hand across his mouth.

"There's a reason why Mr. Boyce hates 'em—a special reason. It has soured his whole disposition. You just as well know about it since Mr. Boyce is your great-uncle. It'll help you understand him better."

Ben stooped to wipe the mud off his knife in the grass. He looked Dan straight in the eye.

"Mr. Boyce had a chestnut mare—a beauty—named Jewel. She had Arabian blood. He was crazy about her. One night last year, Gaunch broke down our corral gate and stole Jewel. Took her with him to live in the wild. She was wearin' a halter at the time but that made no difference to that stud. He would have taken her if she'd been wearin' a full set of harness. He's very determined. He wanted her and he took her.

"Mr. Boyce spent half a year lookin' for her. But nobody has ever seen Jewel alive since. Six months later, a Triangle-D cowboy said he thought he found her body in the mountain down slash. But he didn't see anything of the halter."

Ben pointed to the corral gate. "That's the same gate that stud battered down. We had to rebuild it. See them new timbers?"

"Whew!" said Dan. "He must be big and powerful to have torn through that."

Ben shook his head. "No, sir," he said, "he's not. He's small and feisty. That knot-headed little devil weighs only about nine hundred and fifty pounds. But he's tough and smart and mean.

"He's a vicious fighter, too. He'll charge a mounted man and try to run right over him. He'll rear up on his hind feet and strike at you with his front feet. He can bite a rawhide reata in two. He can run at full speed, driving his band ahead of him, through rough country that would stop any ranch hoss that ever lived."

Dan blinked. He'd heard of wild stallions, but never in such rich detail as Ben pictured this one.

"Why would he want to come way down out of the hills just to steal Jewel?" he asked. "Wasn't there enough mares in his own band?"

"Huh!" chuckled Ben, folding his knife and slipping it into his pocket. "I'll tell you why. Jewel was the handsomest mare on the range. She had looks and class and personality. Intelligent head, ears that stood straight up, bright eyes, clean neck, good flat legs. Her face was straight; she shore wasn't roman-nosed. She carried her tail high. When she dropped it, it fell clear down to her heels.

"She was unshod. Her hoofs were hard as iron. She had wonderful speed and staying power. Once when Mr. Boyce was ridin' her, he could tell she wanted to run. So he let her. She ran three miles at sustained speed and wanted to go further when he pulled her up."

Ben took off his hat and let the wind blow through his red hair, cooling it. His voice grew softer.

"She and Mr. Boyce were great friends. When he called her, she came as fast as she could. She liked him to touch her—back of the ears, along the neck. She liked for him to rub her back. She liked the raisins he fed her. She'd eat 'em off his hand. He always bought several boxes of raisins, when the sup-

26

ply wagon went to town. She was the only horse he ever wanted to ride."

Ben was frowning down at his hands, spreading his fingers. A pause, then he looked up suddenly.

"Mrs. Boyce was a school teacher," he went on. "At first, she was afraid of hosses. Mr. Boyce taught her to ride Jewel. Jewel was gentle as a kitten with her. If she felt Mrs. Boyce slidin' off, she'd slow down 'til Mrs. Boyce wiggled back on."

For the first time, Dan felt a pang of sympathy for the old man. He saw, now, why his great-uncle hated all wild horses. Every time he saw one it reminded him of how he'd lost his beloved mare. He had never gotten over it, probably never would.

Summer passed. With the coming of September, Nevada was still abloom with wild iris in the meadows and wild peach blossoms along the roads. Dan liked to stand outdoors in the morning and draw long lungfuls of the land's fragrance. He liked to feast his eyes on the sunny sagebrush valleys that ran in graceful sweeps toward the mountains.

In late afternoon, before the evening milking, Dan liked to go out into the pasture. He liked to watch his colt race across the meadow, flushing the field larks from their worm hunting. Chico got along well with the other colts. He liked to visit them. He would touch them gently with his nose as if asking after their health and welfare.

In races with the larger colts, the grulla would burst from a standing start like an exploding cork from a champagne bottle.

"He beats those other colts as far as I can throw a rock," Dan told Ben, proudly.

"He wants to win," said Ben, the first time he saw Chico's pasture races. "No matter how much speed a hoss has, he's got to have that 'want to.' He's got to have that old desire." Ben thumped his knuckles against the left side of his own chest. "It's all in here," he added. "It's all in his heart."

Dan even enjoyed watching Chico fight off the flies that bit so cruelly. Without stopping his feeding, Chico would shake his head, wiggle his ears and nip at his own shoulders and flanks. Or with one hind foot, he would scratch behind his ear like a dog while balancing himself on three legs.

He would ripple his neck and stamp his feet. Always his stub tail was sweeping busily up and down or from side to side, as he warded off the pests. And Dan wondered where in the world a colt so young had learned so many ways of defending himself from the attacks of the insect hordes?

Best of all, Dan liked the alert way his colt moved. When Chico walked, he walked at a fast, brisk gait. When he trotted, he trotted fast and smartly. When he ran, he ran awfully fast.

Whenever he started to move in any way, his head was always up to see where he was going. It was part of him. It all went together. In Dan's opinion, it set Chico apart from all the other colts on the ranch.

Soon it became the boy's habit to open a gate and take the foal with him about the ranch. Usually it followed him like a dog. If he saw it was wandering into mischief, he had only to whistle shrilly between his teeth. Chico would come running.

The colt liked apples. With that fruit so plentiful on the ranch, Dan liked to carry apples in his pocket so that he could treat the orphan occasionally.

Only Chico didn't seem like an orphan now. He was growing. When Dan left him in the corral, he was tall enough to stand with his head over the gate, watching Dan as long as he was in sight.

One morning when Dan came in from milking, he couldn't find Chico in either the pony pasture or the corral.

"Chico!" he called. "Where are you?"

From the depths of the barn came the colt's eager whinny. Dan grinned. He called again. Guided by the colt's neighing, he kept approaching nearer and nearer. Then Dan saw the mustang in the semi-darkness of the stall.

"There you are, Chico!" he called. Chico continued to neigh but kept softening the tone until when Dan stood by his side at last, his whicker was as tender as the cooing of a dove.

Stretching out a hand, Dan passed it over the foal's smooth flank and up to the face which he pulled over against his own, talking to him all the while. And Dan thought, I sure like you. I like everything about you. Especially do I like your soft breathing when I put my head next to yours.

And the hurt was gone forever from Dan Deweese's heart, the hurt brought on by the stepfather's greed and rascality.

Forewarned that a colt's first winter is his most crucial time, Dan asked questions right and left. He listened thoughtfully to all the answers. Although the corral shed's north wall blocked off the icy wind and all the other colts apparently were comfortable there, when the weather grew severe Dan would sometimes smuggle his foal into the barn.

On these occasions he would fork down plenty of dry straw, as the floors were cold. Twice each day he haltered his pet and led him to water. In addition to oats, he began feeding Chico prairie hay for roughage.

But the grulla seemed to thrive in any kind of weather. Soon Dan stopped coddling him. Running remained the youngster's favorite sport. No matter what the condition of the ground, Chico ran off from the bigger ranch colts in their sprints from fence to fence.

When November's snows came, Dan gave Chico plenty of daytime exercise in the pony pasture. Even with the weather around zero and the snow eight

inches deep, Dan kept him out in it for an hour each day. And the leggy stripling liked it.

When Tonia offered to heat the colt's drinking water to take the chill off it, Dan accepted. However, he doubted if the kindness was needed. Apparently the colt paid no attention to the cold.

The weather changed. On an afternoon of warmth and sunshine, old Buck saw the water warming on the kitchen range.

"What you heatin' the water fer?" he asked.

"For Chico, *señor*," Tonia replied. It was the first time she had called the colt by that name. Dan, standing nearby after fetching the water from the well, was secretly pleased.

"Humpf!" grunted the old man. "Why you need so much? You gonna give him a tub bath or somethin'?"

"No, *señor* Boyce," said Tonia. "It's for him to drink."

"Humpf," fussed old Buck. "Next you'll be bringin' that wild thing into the house to spend the night."

Tonia just looked pleasant and continued to busy herself at the stove.

"How would you like to have apple pie for supper tonight, *señor*?" She tossed the remark carelessly over her shoulder while peeling apples at the cabinet.

The old man lost his sour look. His eyes gleamed with at least the faint beginnings of good humor.

"You know I like apple pie," he said.

Tonia said, "I'm running a little behind today. If I can find some way to cool the pie, we'll have it for supper tonight."

When the pie was baked, Tonia raised the kitchen window and set the pie on the sill to cool. Then she promptly forgot all about it.

Chico, prowling the yard, spied it. Five minutes later, when Tonia remembered to go get it, she shrank

31

back from the disaster at the window. With a cry, she threw up both hands.

"*Madre de Dios!*"

Chico was finishing off the last of the pie, his head plunged almost up to his eyes in its spicy goodness.

Tonia, very embarrassed, apologized to old Buck.

"I'll bake you another tomorrow, *señor*," she promised.

"Don't leave it in the window next time," the old man growled. "Just bring it to me hot."

He jerked his chair out from the table. "I'm gonna quit givin' that danged little broomtail the run of the whole ranch," he added as he sat down to a supper at which no dessert was served. "That's gonna stop right now."

Later, when Tonia told Dan about it, the boy's sober face melted into one of his rare smiles. Before he went to bed, he walked to the corral to pat his foal and talk to him.

"You got us in trouble, chum," Dan told the colt. "Uncle Buck called you a pie-biter. He says I've got to keep you out of the ranch yard."

When he left, Chico went with him to the fence and stood quietly with his head over the top wire, watching him out of sight.

A week later somebody left a gate unlatched and two of the ranch's saddle horses joined the wild bunch that roamed the distant hills.

Dan was awakened in the middle of the night by what sounded like a wild horse's shrill neigh. As he ran barefoot to the corral, he heard Chico answer the call with what Dan imagined to be a longing nicker of his own.

Quickly, Dan ran to him. "Who were you talkin' to?" he asked the colt. "Cut it out! Don't get any wild notions! You're stayin' right here with me."

Chico only looked at him mildly and went on chewing the hay.

A Matter of Balance

To Dan, ranch life was fascinating. He was delighted when Ben assigned him two mounts to ride, both small breeds. Now that he was outgrowing the clothing that Tonia had given him, he wanted to learn all about the business of being a cowpuncher.

"All right, kid," said Ben when the boy broached the subject to him. "Some guys become punchers right off, others never do. We'll find out what you can learn."

Dan Boyce learned. Ben eased him into it gradually. He started him off plowing fire-guards, two parallel sets of furrows so that the grass between them could be purposely burned by men accompanied by water wagons. He set him to inspecting and repairing fence, and loose-herding the remuda where the grass grew greenest and best.

Dan learned other things, too. Ben showed him how to wrangle horses, how to pull mired cattle from bog holes, how to track cattle that had strayed too far afield and turn them back, and how to fork hay down from stacks to the animals in winter. Dan grew leaner and tougher. His skin became brown as calf leather.

But he still cut and gathered wood for Tonia and

Carmen besides doing lifting for each around the house. He realized that he wasn't yet big enough or skilled enough to be a top hand, although Ben once told him, "Yore gainin' on it."

Hungrier than ever now that he was working harder, Dan liked eating in the cook house.

"What we havin' tonight?" he once asked Carmen.

"Beef," she replied, adjusting the damper of the kitchen range.

Dan said, "I thought we had beef last night. Or was it pork?"

"It was ham, *señor!*" said Carmen. And Dan thought, "They sure put out lots of meat at this ranch. 'Line a cowboy's ribs with it and he'll give you fifteen hours of work a day' must be Uncle Buck's motto."

Dan asked, "When we gonna have pancakes?"

Carmen looked horrified. "Never, I hope," she said, "They too much trouble. I can't cook that fast for fifteen men!"

Dan blinked, trying to imagine how busy Carmen would be flipping forty-five pancakes at once. Abashed, he blew out his breath. She was right. He had never looked at it before from the cook's viewpoint.

The saddle Ben had lent him was far too big. Even after Ben shortened the stirrups, Dan bounced all over it.

Next morning after breakfast, sad-faced José came to the bunkhouse carrying a small saddle and a blanket. The saddle, a Heiser, had a high horn. It was almost new.

"It was Chico's," said José, "but he never got to use it very much."

He helped Dan put the saddle on Freddie, one of the horses assigned to him.

"It's yours, *señor* Dan, if you want it," José said in what seemed a long speech for him. "Ever time Tonia look at it I think she's gonna cry. So it's better for you to have it."

Dan's eyes grew so big you could have roped them with a grapevine.

"Oh, thank you," he said. He climbed on Freddie. "Fits fine. I'll sure take good keer of it."

Dan was so proud of that saddle that he seldom let it touch the ground. After the day's work was over, he was careful to hang it on the rack. Although the night was clear and it hadn't rained for weeks, before Dan went to bed he found an old piece of tarp and covered the saddle carefully.

I can't wait to slip it on Chico, he thought. *I'll bet it will fit him, too.* But Chico was too young to ride.

With the coming of spring, Chico began shedding his winter hair. Now almost a year old, the colt stood still as stone while Dan, using a curry comb, raked off the old hair in big bunches.

"Your new hair is growin' underneath," Dan told the colt. "It's brighter and shinier."

Then early in summer, the colt started putting on his winter coat. Gradually, his hair became coarser, longer, and shaggier.

"By October, you'll be like a man wearing a beaver overcoat," Dan told him. "You'll never get cold."

Meanwhile, the boy discovered that Ben had put him on the ranch payroll.

"Les go by the big white house a minute an' see Mr. Boyce," Ben said mysteriously one morning. They followed the other cowhands onto the wide porch and into the sitting room where Uncle Buck was huddled behind his desk. Only the old man's eyes and shiny dome were visible over several neat piles of silver dollars stacked in front of him.

Dan caught his breath in awe and licked his lips. He had never seen so much money at one time. As fast as one cowhand stepped up, Uncle Buck counted out thirty of the coins and dropped them into each man's palm, five at a time.

Dan was given twenty of them. Thrilled by their weight in his hand, he blurted, "Thank you, sir." But Uncle Buck just grunted and went on paying the others.

Ben said, "I tried to get Mr. Boyce to pay 'em off in bank notes. It'd be lots easier. But he don't like bank notes. Calls 'em 'California money.' Like everybody else in Nevada, he prefers these silver cartwheels."

On his first trip to town, Dan spent a month's salary for a new pair of high heeled boots. They had pull-on straps at the top that Ben called "mule ears."

Dan's education, or lack of it, had also become a problem. The boy had been a fifth-grader before running off to Nevada. He wanted to learn.

In the parlor of the ranch house Mrs. Boyd had kept a small library. In it, Ben found an arithmetic manual, a blueback speller and a *Curry's Literary Reader*. Each of them was well worn. At night, Dan borrowed them and tried to teach himself. But it was slow going. In Nevada in 1915, there was very little schooling in the ranching areas.

Then Ben had an idea. "Mrs. Tandy, in town, used to teach a private school before she married Thurman," he told old Buck. "Why don't the boy ride over and see her twice a month? He could get our letters at the post office and have her hear his lessons. He could stay overnight with them. We could send them a beef as payment."

Old Buck didn't look too happy about it. But Ben was his foreman and a good one. The old man had to listen to him.

So it was agreed. Every two weeks Dan rode Rollie, the older cow pony, into the pleasant tree-shaded town of Elko, carrying his books in one saddle pocket and bringing back the ranch mail in the other. While in town, he began writing letters to his mother back in Nebraska. The railroad ran through Elko, and his letters, as well as hers in reply, moved promptly.

Most displeased of all with the new arrangement was Chico. Each time Dan rode off on Rollie, the wild colt ran down the fence line with them until the road turned north. Then he stood under a small mesquite tree watching them out of sight. And Dan thought, *I'll sure be glad when you're old enough to ride.*

Dan sat on the corral fence watching old Buck's cowhands ride a young bronco. The corral was round so the bronco couldn't pin the riders in a corner. In its exact center was planted a strong snubbing post. A high log fence was built all around. The cowboys called the top rail the "op'ra house" because it was the best seat from which to watch the bucking.

"Ben, when you gonna let me try one of them jug-heads?" Dan asked when the foreman walked by. He was looking to the time he could be a full-blown cow-hand at thirty-five dollars per month. He knew that every cowboy had to learn to ride bucking horses. If he couldn't, the whole ranch soon would know about it. The boss would probably hire somebody else.

Ben frowned. "All right," he said. "But first les talk about it. Why don't you drop by my house tonight after supper?"

Dan did. Sitting on the foreman's concrete back step, he listened while Ben talked.

"I think you've got a good build for it but it goes lots further than that," Ben said. "The best bronc rid-ers ain't very big. Very few men get hurt ridin' the ranch buckers."

Ben lifted his chin and spat a brown tobacco stream over a creosote bush nearby.

"First, les look at it from the hoss's angle," he went on. "Every hoss bucks now an' then. It's natural with 'em. They get it from their ancestors I guess. In the old days, when a cougar or a lion jumped on their back, the first thing a hoss did was try to buck him off. I once had a mare with four claw marks on her right hip. A lion had jumped off a rock onto her. She

37

was awful touchy about lettin' anything get behind her after that."

Ben wiped his hand across his mouth. "Ridin' ranch hosses is lots easier than ridin' rodeo hosses," he said. "We try to break these ranch hosses without makin' 'em buckers. Then something will touch 'em off. But they usually just buck a little and turn out to be good cow hosses."

"Yeah, but how do I stay on one?" asked Dan, impatiently.

"You won't always stay on," said Ben. "ever'body kisses the ground now and then. Ridin' broncs is a matter of balance, not physical strength. You float with the hoss. You ride above the seat of your saddle. You learn to stand in the stirrups to avoid the rough poundin' and jarrin'."

He spat again, this time spraying a green cactus under the clothesline.

"You gotta have guts, too," he went on. "A bronc rider has either got 'em or he ain't got 'em. Main thing is not to let the boss know you're scared of him or he'll end up lickin' you. He can tell right off. I think you'll do all right."

Next morning in the corral, Dan got his chance. He was determined to do well. They led out a smallish black gelding. While a cowboy wearing green gloves stood at the horse's head holding a sack over the animal's eyes to keep him quiet, Dan saddled him.

Ben had shown Dan how to saddle a bronc. "Hook the right stirrup over the saddle horn so it can't flop around," Ben said, "an' bring both cinches over the top of the saddle so they won't get in the way. Then ease the saddle on him. Move it around. Settle it."

Most of old Buck's cowhands were perched on the corral's top rail, like chickadees on a telegraph line. Their advice came from all directions.

"Don't be bashful about pullin' leather," shouted Tex Tolbert, who wore a yellow neckerchief around

his sunburned neck. "Grab the saddlehorn. Grab anything. Grab him round the neck if you have to."

Dan grasped the saddle horn with one hand and the cantle with the other. Placing his left foot in the stirrup, he rocked up and down a couple of times as he had seen the others do.

The black shied nervously. *He's as scared as I am*, Dan told himself. *We're both scared spitless.*

Earl Stains, a tall frown-faced cowboy who wore goatskin chaps, yelled: "Roller his head, Little Podnuh! Watch his head an' ears or he'll slide out from under you. Most of 'em buck with their head between their forelegs. Long as you can see his ears, you can stay on him."

Dan swung lightly into the saddle and thrust his feet into the stirrups.

"When you feel yourself fallin' kick free of the stirrups, so he can't drag you by one leg," Seth

Shannon called out. "You'll know a jump or two ahead when yore gonna fall. Go limp an' hit the ground rollin'."

José added, "An' don' let him step on you."

Annoyed, Dan took a firm grip on the reins. *He's not going to step on me because I'm not going to be bucked off,* he vowed to himself.

But he was excited nevertheless. He wished they would keep their advice to themselves. He thought, *how am I ever going to be able to think about all this when the bronc starts pitching and my brains are knocked down into the seat of my pants?*

Then the green-gloved cowboy whipped the sack off the black's head and fanned him with it, yelling loudly. Dan raked the black with his spurs.

The horse jumped forward. To Dan's astonishment, it began pacing around and around the corral, like a harness horse circling the track at a county fair.

"Scratch him with yore spurs!" somebody yelled.

"Hit him with your hat!" shouted another.

Although Dan did both those things, and more, the horse refused to buck. He just kept running. Finally a hazer ran out and stopped him. Dan got off.

He felt disgusted and let down, as if he'd been cheated out of something he wanted very much. He didn't know what to do or whom to blame.

Five minutes later he got another chance. A wiry little paint was brought out and subdued while Dan saddled him. Dan swung up on him. He set his feet in the stirrups.

"Turn him loose!" he yelled and braced himself.

Freed, the paint boiled over. He bucked like a pump handle going up and down. He landed on his front feet, then on his hind feet. Dan was off guard. He wasn't ready. He'd been keyed up good for the black. But he hadn't had time to point for the paint.

Excited, Dan forgot all the excellent advice given him. Even then, he rode the paint three or four seconds. Soon, he became unbalanced and knew he was going off. For a moment, the boy was airborne. Then the ground came up and met him roughly.

Dazed, Dan got to his knees. He shook his brown head vigorously. *The only thing I did right was roll,* he remembered ruefully.

"Lemme try him again!" he said hotly, scrambling to his feet. "I can ride him! I know I can!" He was surprised how easy it had been.

Ben Dragoo came up, his white teeth bared in a grin. "You already rode him several jumps," he said. "That's enough fer now. We might try him again tomorrow."

To his surprise, the old man's cowhands heaped considerable praise on him.

"Nice ridin', little podnuh," said Earl Stains. "You set him as easy as a hoss fly on a mule's ear."

"Good ride!" said Lee Rawson, his blond mustache bobbing up and down, "even if you did end up walkin.'"

"With yore hind legs kickin' around in the air you looked like a migratin' bull-frog in full flight," kidded Tex Tolbert, "but you got some talent, all right."

Thus passed Dan Deweese's first effort at the stirring art of horse breaking.

We Live Like Moles

From that beginning, Dan learned the duties of a cowboy as well as those of a chore boy. His improvement came slow but steady.

How to throw a rope gave him the most trouble. With Ben along to advise him, Dan bought a light thirty-five-foot coil of manila hemp next time they went to town.

"José will show you how to throw it," said Ben. "He's one of our best ropers. As a boy he started droppin' loops over dogs, chickens, geese—anything on the place that offered a target."

With José advising him, Dan spent much of his spare time hurling the rope. Casting a six-foot loop twenty feet through the air around the neck of a running cow or calf, when he himself was mounted on a speeding pony, was the most difficult thing that Dan had ever tried to do.

He did learn that ropes have many practical values. They could be used to fasten unruly broncs to the snubbing post. They were handy for yanking a mired cow by her horns from a bog hole, although once she was free she might charge and try to hook you. When doubled, a rope became an excellent quirt with which to kill rattlesnakes or rouse a balky steer.

When Dan went after stove wood for Tonia and Carmen, or a load of logs for old Buck's fireplace, he dragged it home with his rope fastened to his saddle horn. The boy spent much of his spare time trying to throw his rope. Soon he wished that he could practice with it full time, so slowly did his skill improve.

But it did improve, and so did his other cowboy skills.

The days passed into weeks and the weeks into months, and at last the hour came when Chico's mouse-colored body had grown in proportion to his eyes and legs. It was time to break him to ride. Dan had carefully collected riding information from everybody who would talk to him about it.

He started in the Indian way, by leaning on his walking colt and gradually putting more and more weight on his sensitive back. Then he put a blanket on him, then his empty saddle, making him graze and drink while wearing both about the ranch. He had long since introduced him to the bit.

As a horse fears nothing to which it is accustomed, Dan let Chico see, touch, and smell everything before he put it on him. He even hung straps, chains, and tin cans to the saddle and let them dangle against Chico's hocks and knees so that he was never startled by sudden noises behind him.

For months Dan had been aware of his horse's muscular development. It explained Chico's fast start and withering speed. Although he was small and trim, the grulla was muscled in the right places, in the upper part of his forelegs coming down off his shoulders, and in the upper part of his hind legs coming down off his hips.

He had to get that from his breeding, Dan reasoned. From his forebears, he had also got his "want to," as Ben called it—his desire to excel in every race he ever ran. Dan wished with all his heart that he knew who the grulla's ancestors had been.

To Dan's utter amazement, the first time he climbed on Chico's back, the mustang dropped his head between his front legs and bucked him off.

It happened in the horse pasture where Dan had led him by the bridle, then mounted. But instead of running off and leaving Dan to walk home, Chico stood and waited until the boy got up.

"You're a fine partner," Dan scolded him gently, seizing the dangling reins. "Why didn't you give me a little warning?"

Chico turned around and looked at him. Then he moved closer and nosed Dan gently. Dan grinned. "I still like you," he said, "even if you did make me chew grass."

Again Dan mounted. Again Chico pitched, flattening his ears and humping his back. He made several stiff-legged bone-jarring bounds. But this time Dan was ready. He rode him easily, talking to him all the while.

Realizing that the boy was there to stay, Chico stopped trying to unseat him and paced around and

around the pasture. Dan directed him by shifting the reins to the left side of his neck when he wanted him to turn left, and to the right when he wished him to go right.

"He's easy to ride," Dan told Ben Dragoo later. "He's got good shoulders and a good back. The saddle fits him good. He's sure-footed, too. He runs with his nose to the ground and his eyes glued on the trail. His gait is smooth and silky."

"Just like my old grulla," grinned Ben. "I told you that the wild ones make the best cow ponies."

"He catches on to things awfully fast," Dan added.

That remark fit the little mustang like the skin on a green sand plum. Chico was maturing into a most intelligent cow horse. In only his second round-up, he showed what he had learned.

Since it was old Buck Boyce's business to raise

and sell thousands of cattle, he had to be sure that the ones he sold belonged to him and wore his Bar-B brand. During the spring roundup, all the Bar-B cattle became mixed together on the range with those of neighboring ranchers. It was the duty of the Bar-B cowboys to separate them from the general mass wearing many different brands. Then they could be grouped in a special area.

Soon it became Dan's habit to read from a distance the brands of every cow he came across. He had no trouble recognizing the brand on a Bar-B animal. But extricating him from the tightly-massed herd wearing several brands was a different matter. This was where Chico shone. He seemed to take as much interest in this work as did his rider.

The grulla could not read the brands burned on the cattle's hips, sides, and shoulders. But when Dan showed him by steering him in pursuit of it which animal he wanted cut out, Chico would follow it without being told by anybody.

A spotted steer was defying the efforts of some of old Buck's cowboys to cut him from the herd.

Ben Dragoo rode up to Dan. "Wanta take a run at that cactus-boomer?" he called, sleeving the sweat from his forehead. "Looks like he don' wanna be cut."

Dan moved Chico in behind the spotted outlaw and let the little horse take over. Trailing him at a slow walk so as not to alarm the others, Chico herded him to the outskirts.

Then the spotted steer discovered that he was being parted from his companions. Quickly, he tried to break back among them, his tail hoisted in the air. A young range-raised steer can run like a deer.

With Dan encouraging him with sharp yells, Chico flew at the runaway. With bursts of scorching speed, he always stayed between him and the main body. No matter how many times the spotted steer tried to rejoin his fellows, Chico always cut him off.

Controlling him with ease, the grulla drove him back into the Bar-B herd.

Dan was delighted at how quickly his colt had learned this cutting skill.

"He makes 'em go where I want 'em to go, not where they want to go," he told Earl Stains, proudly.

Stains nodded. "A good cuttin' pony is a scarce article," he said. "They can turn on a quarter and give you back fifteen cents in change."

And Dan wished with all his heart that his great-uncle had been there to see the incident and hear what the tall cowboy said.

A week after the roundup, on a morning desolate with rain, old Buck sat in his rocker in front of the fireplace in the sitting room of the ranch house.

With a broom and mop, Tonia was cleaning the room. Dan was picking up the elk hides and wolf skins on the floor, carrying them out on the porch to be shaken and aired.

The old man wore one of his sour looks. He seemed to be listening to the crackle of the burning logs inside and to the moaning of the wind outside.

"Don't get up, *señor* Boyce," said Tonia, politely. "I can clean around you. Just raise your feet— please—so I can get under them. It won't take a minute."

Obediently, the old man raised his boots while grasping the rungs of the chair.

"No use cleaning up in this room," he said, gloomily.

"We live like moles out here. Nobody ever comes to see us."

No wonder, thought Dan, as he carried the bucket of suds for Tonia. You're so mean and grouchy that nobody wants to come around you.

Sympathy shone in Tonia's kind face. "It's a long way out to this ranch, *señor* Boyce," she said. "We'd have more visitors if we lived closer to town."

48

"We used to have lots of company anyhow," growled the old man, still holding his feet up.

Tonia worked fast. "Now you can put them down, *señor*," she said. The old man's boots clumped to the floor.

Dan helped Tonia move a heavy oaken table and thought about it. *Sounds like he's lonely*, the boy told himself. *I'll bet he used to enjoy guests. Wonder what's happened to change him? Does he miss his wife? Or is he still saddened because the wild stud stole Jewel?*

Next morning, the old man did something that surprised Dan greatly. He saddled a horse and rode to town instead of going in the buggy or the supply wagon. But it was what he did after he got there that amazed Dan.

Ben Dragoo went with him. Earl Stains was left in charge at the ranch.

"They're gonna look at some mares that Mr. Boyce might buy," Stains explained at dinner. "Mr. Boyce is prepared to spend several thousand dollars for 'em if he finds what he's lookin' for. He plans to upgrade his hoss stock, go for class."

Five days later, they returned driving six blooded mares of the steeldust breed. Dan stared at them in admiration. They had beautiful bodies and intelligent heads. They were noted for their ability to survive on short food in bad weather. And they could run.

"Mr. Boyce is gonna breed 'em to a quarter horse stallion," Ben told Dan.

Proud of the mettlesome mares, the old man seemed to recover some of his former vigor. He combed them, patted them, and petted them. He fed them apples from the bin.

"Whoa now, lady," he would say gently and soothingly when he approached them one by one with a brush. "Let me clean you up."

Dan thought, he sure knows how to talk to them and to make them like him.

They soon grew to know him, too. They would nudge him, looking for apples. And the shine came back into the old man's eye. His step became lighter and quicker.

The fall roundup followed in September. It was then that the late calves were branded. The beeves that had strayed to the rougher country were found so they could be gathered and shipped.

Dan, on Chico, had flushed a yellow steer in a canyon. It had wide horns. For an hour it defied all their efforts to drive it out. Finally, they herded it back onto the range. Both Dan and Chico were very tired.

The steer was stubborn and contrary. It broke down a gully at full speed. Dan sent Chico after it. Chico quickly overhauled it but the footing was rough. Dan was content to tail it closely for the moment. Both animals were running hard.

Suddenly, the steer stepped in a prairie dog hole and fell sprawling, all twelve-hundred pounds of him, directly in front of Chico. Dan gasped and set himself, expecting the worst fall of his life.

Instead, he felt himself lifting and soaring. Alert and sure-footed in the crisis, Chico, without breaking stride, had jumped entirely over the steer.

The animal got to its feet, but now Chico was behind it. He had the position he wanted. Wheeling, he drove it back at a trot toward the wagon.

"Good boy!" said Dan, soon as he got over his fright. Reaching down, he patted his pet on the neck. "That's the way to jump 'em, chum," he said. "That's the way to swap ends, too." More cowboys are badly hurt by falling horses than by any other means, he'd heard Ben say.

When they got back to the ranch, Dan told about Chico's leap to everybody who would listen.

Chico had also become a good roping horse. This was the hardest and most dangerous cattle work of all. When Dan roped a calf or a yearling steer to be

50

branded, the work had just begun. José showed Dan how to make the rope sing, to flow freely through the loop with a hissing sound.

After the catch, before the rope tightened, the boy learned to take a couple of quick turns of the rope's home end around his saddle horn. This was called a dally. Then with his left hand, Dan would pull lightly back on the reins and Chico would sit back, hind feet planted under him, fore feet braced well out in front, and receive the shock. Jose had taught Dan this roping trick.

When the steer came to the end of the rope, he was jerked off his feet and fell heavily. Then it was Chico's job to back up or otherwise keep the rope tight until the cowboys could move in with the hot branding iron and quickly stamp the Bar-B on the left side of the animal's back, behind the shoulder.

Before they learned the knack, Chico and Dan suffered two rough falls. Both times, Chico did not plant his feet firmly and brace himself in time to meet the shock.

"No wonder you got fooled," said Dan, picking himself up painfully off the ground. "You were so surprised at me finally catching something with my rope that you didn't know how to act. You hadn't had that kind of experience." But Chico soon learned.

"He's all business," Dan told Ben later. He's easy to handle, too. When you take him out of the stall in the morning, he's ready to walk, gallop, work cattle— whatever you want him to do. He catches on to things awfully fast."

A week later, Dan rode to town to get the mail and let Mrs. Tandy hear his lessons. Now fourteen years old, he was doing eighth grade work. Since he had pushed Chico hard in the roundups, he rode Freddie and left Chico behind in the horse pasture to rest. But Chico didn't want to rest.

The little mustang ran down the fence line, nickering with disappointment. When Dan, on Freddie, turned north, Chico stood miserably at the fence, staring at them until they passed from sight.

On Dan's return trip two days later, Ben Dragoo, on his fastest horse, met him at a point five miles from the ranch.

"Dan, I've got bad news for you," said Ben, pulling with both hands to rein in his mount. "Gaunch, the wild stud, stole all six of Mr. Boyce's steeldust mares last night. Tex Tolbert saw him bitin' 'em and kickin' 'em and makin' 'em go with him. The stud an' his band also took some of our best saddle horses."

Ben's bay, nervous and hot, pranced in a slow circle as Ben again swung him around, facing Dan. There was sympathy in Ben's face and a strange reluctance in his manner.

"One of the hosses they took was your pony, Chico," he said.

Trouble at the Bar-B

Dan rode back to the ranch in a daze, hardly seeing the dusty trail. He felt a dull ache, a bitter grief, a sense of hopelessness and despair.

He tried to think what life would be like without Chico. *He was all I had in the world*, Dan told himself. *I liked him so well.* To have a colt he could groom, fondle, talk to and love blindly was the greatest happiness the boy had ever known.

He found the ranch in turmoil, all because of the depredations of one small stud. Everybody looked and acted as if a tornado had struck or the place had been plundered by outlaws.

The calmest person there, and also the maddest, was old Buck Boyce. His eyes had narrowed to slits of blue-green fire. But he was acting coolly and swiftly in the crisis. He wasn't going to take this lying down.

"We're goin' after 'em," he growled, "even if it breaks the bank and we have to chase 'em clear to Montana."

Already he had dispatched Bar-B riders in all directions.

José was gone in a supply wagon to a neighbor's for axes and wire. Ben was winging his way to town for the horse doctor. Earl Stains was riding to Balko to fetch Pete Wano.

"Who's Pete Wano?" Dan heard somebody ask.

"The best mustanger in Nevada," said Seth Shannon. "He makes his livin' trappin' wild hosses."

Dan caught his breath and felt a flash of hope. Maybe they'd all get their horses back yet. He was still so stunned and heartbroken that he couldn't eat any supper.

Later, Tonia called him to the ranch house kitchen. With her white apron, she dusted off a chair. She gave him one of her kind smiles.

"Sit down, *señor* Dan," she said, "and see what I baked for you."

When she brought him a slab of hot apple pie fresh from her oven, Dan nearly broke down. He remembered how Chico had stuck his head in the window and demolished that other apple pie.

Tonia understood at once. "Oh *señor* Dan," she said in tones of deep remorse, "I should have remembered. I am very sorry."

Dan blinked, the unshed tears aching behind his eyes. He sniffed once and thought, *I'm acting like a child about all this. I've got to toughen up, get my nerve back.*

He tried to smile but couldn't. "It sure smells good," he mumbled. "Give me a fork, please."

Tonia hurried to the cabinet to get one.

Later, Dan asked Seth Shannon, "How did Gaunch get the mares out of the corral? That new corral gate is made of green logs."

"They wasn't in the corral," said Shannon. "They was out on the open range for one night only. They was to be driven to another range. Tex Tolbert was ridin' night herd on 'em. That's when the brown stud hit 'em—at sundown. I don't know how he found out.

"When Tex tried to take the steeldusts away from him, the stud ran right at him with his mouth open. He reared up on his hind legs and pawed the air. He tried to take down Tex's mount. He tried to grab Tex with his teeth."

54

Dan also learned why Ben had gone after the horse doctor.

"The quarter horse stallion the boss was gonna breed the steeldusts to was shut up in the feed lot," Lee Rawson said. "He challenged Gaunch and tried to get at him. That little brown devil saved him the trouble. He broke down the feed lot plank gate and nearly killed the quarter horse stallion. He kicked in several of his ribs. He chewed big bites of flesh out of his neck. He almost bit off one ear."

Dan went to the barn to look at the quarter horse stallion. The proud beast stood trembling in its stall, its wounds still open and untended. Dan felt no admiration for the wild stud, only hate.

At the barn next afternoon, old Buck was making plans and giving orders.

"They got Danny Deweese's pony Chico, too," somebody said.

The old man whirled round, glaring at the speaker. "Good riddance!" he barked. "I'm glad that danged little fuzztail's gone. That's where he belongs—back up in the greasewood with his folks."

Dan's small jaw set firmly. He felt his temper rising. Although he doubted old Buck knew he was anywhere around to hear, the words hurt anyhow.

Next morning, Pete Wano rode in from the desert. A half-breed Shoshone Indian, he was big and brawny with hands as large as pancakes. In his buckskin moccasins, he moved about the ranch with authority and grace. Quickly, he and old Buck moved to the blacksmith shop to talk.

Dan looked with interest at the Indian's horse, a cream-colored coyote dun with a black mane and tail. The horse followed its master like a dog until Wano spoke to it quietly. Then it stood unhappily, gazing at his disappearing form.

Obviously, it worshipped him. And Dan recalled,

with a tug on his own heartstrings, how Chico had dogged him in much the same manner.

Ben Dragoo got back with the horse doctor in mid-afternoon. Old Buck immediately called a general meeting to acquaint everybody with the strategy decided upon.

"This here is Pete Wano, the mustanger," he began. "You've all heared of him. Pete says the best way to catch wild hosses bossed by a stud like Gaunch is to trap 'em when they go to drink." He looked at Wano.

The half breed nodded slowly and solemnly, "That's right, Mr. Boyce," he said. "But they're very hard to trap. Seven times out of ten something usually goes wrong."

Dan was surprised to hear him speak in almost perfect English. He'd gone to college at the Carlisle Indian School in Pennsylvania to play football, Dan found out later.

Wano went on, "Water is very scarce in this part of Nevada. The only water the wild ones can get, besides the moisture from the dew on the grass they eat in the mornings, is from the small springs that flow down from the mountains. But there are only a few such springs—very few. A lot of them have dried up." His voice was musical and deep.

"How do you find the wild hosses in the first place?" Ben Dragoo asked.

Pete Wano faced him courteously. "The Shoshone scouts who help me go to the foothills and find them," he replied. "They are trained men. They've already started scouting this band. Soon as they find it, they come back and tell me. Then we'll go after them."

"How do you find the springs where the fuzzies drink?" somebody else asked.

"We already know the location of all the springs in this part of the country," Wano replied. "There aren't very many. Soon as we find the horses we know where they'll go to drink."

56

Seth Shannon asked, "How you goin' to trap 'em after you find 'em?" Thinking of Chico, Dan could feel his pulse pounding. It was exactly the same question he had wished to ask.

Pete Wano said, "By first building a stockade fence, with wings, around their water hole. Sort of a corral of timber and wire. We pile brush around it so they won't see it. When they come to drink, we drive them into it."

Earl Stains asked, "Won't they smell your odor around the fence?"

Pete Wano nodded. "Probably. And when they first smell it, they might run away. But not very far. They all have to drink, sooner or later. It's very hot now. They have no choice. They must drink, or die of thirst."

"How do you know they'll come to the watering spot you build the fence around?" Tex Tolbert wanted to know.

"We first locate the band without letting them see us," said Pete Wano. "Once we find them, we know where they're going to drink. For each five or six parks or meadows they feed in, there's only one water hole. They're often fifteen to twenty miles apart. We know where they are. We scout the watering holes hardest of all because all the wild bands have to go to them."

Earl Stains rolled himself a cigarette and licked the edge of the paper. "I don't mean to be nosey," he said, "but why do you go after wild hosses in the first place?"

Pete Wano faced him. "Why? To recover quality horses—like Mr. Boyce's steeldust mares—that have been carried off by the wild bands. It's a business with us. The ranchers pay us for recovering their stock. We keep the wild ones and break them to ride. Then we sell them."

Earl Stains said, "How do you know the wild ones won't go someplace else—say a hundred miles off—and find another water hole?"

Wano explained. "A wild band lives nearly all its life on a range no more then twenty miles across," he said. "They never wander from north to south—like buffalo. No matter how far a stallion leader is crowded off his range, he always comes back to it. This brown stallion you all speak of is out there someplace close right now."

"Yeah," muttered old Buck, "an' my steeldusts are out there with him."

The old man looked around. "Any more questions?" he asked. There were none. "All right. We leave in 'bout an hour. We'll pack our own food an' bed rolls an' take 'em with us. We'll water our own hosses heavy now, and on the way—as long as we can. All right. Les go."

After the men scattered, Dan went up to his great-uncle.

"Uncle Buck, kin I go too?" he asked, his eyes pleading. "I want to get my pony back."

The old man frowned. "Why don't you fergit all about that broomtail?" he grumbled. "Let him stay out there in the creosote bushes, like his ma and pa. He'll never amount to a dang here."

Dan stared at him, hotly. "He's already a good cowhorse, Uncle Buck," he said. "He's a fine cuttin' horse, too. Ask Ben or Earl Stains or any of your cowhands. An' he's gettin' to be a good ropin' horse."

The old man snorted in scorn. "Funny I never heared about it," he said. "All he's ever been good for 'round here is to eat up our oats and hay. An' our apple pies," he added spitefully.

"Please, Uncle Buck," begged Dan. "I like him awful well. I want to get him back."

The old man turned away. "I might talk to Ben about it," he flung the words back over his shoulder unwillingly. Then he passed from sight around the corner of the barn.

Dan felt his lips go dry. He wet them with his tongue and decided to take action himself.

Dan talked to Ben about it. Ben was busy but he always listened. Ben talked to old Buck.

"We need a boy to wrangle our extra hosses an' build fence an' do odd jobs, Mr. Boyce!" he said. "This boy does a good job of that. He does a good job at purely everything—except ropin'—an' he's learnin' that. The day is soon comin' when we'll have to pay him thirty-five a month."

So Dan went, riding Rollie and leading Freddie with his bedding tied behind the saddle.

All day they traveled at a fast walk. Pete Wano scouted ahead, following the tracks of the stallion and his band through the sage. The hoof prints of the six steeldust mares were easy to find because they wore iron shoes.

"It's best to go slow all the way to their water hole," Dan heard Pete Wano explain to old Buck, "and keep our horses fresh for the hard running that is sure to come when we jump them." To Dan, it made good sense.

"What we do, we have to do when we first jump them," Wano went on. "We have to surprise them. These wild horses have great stamina. I have known them to gallop several miles, then spurt and run off from the fresh horses sent against them."

Although the expedition was moving, Pete Wano got no rest from the questions put up by the Bar-B hands. Dan listened eagerly. It was a fascinating subject.

"Do ranch horses ever join a wild bunch of their own free will?" Lee Rawson asked.

"Yes," replied the Shoshone. "A tame horse just naturally likes to join a wild bunch. He's curious to find out what goes on in one. It's an exciting life. I think he likes the freedom he sees in the wild ones. He likes the companionship, too."

59

Dan thought that Chico would never join them for that reason. *We always gave each other plenty of companionship*, he told himself. But he worried about it anyhow.

"What makes wild hosses so tough?" Seth Shannon wanted to know.

Wano's eyes flashed darkly. "Because only the strongest and fastest of them survive," he said. "For years, they've been shot at, and trapped, and killed off. The weak ones, the slow ones, and the scrubs are all gone. Only the tough ones remain. This has improved the breed. It's harder than ever to capture them today."

"How do they stay alive in winter?" Earl Stains asked.

"For one thing, they're never thirsty in winter," said Wano. "They drink the snow. Getting food is harder, but they manage. Ponies can pick up a living where cattle die. After the first frosts cure the white sage, they eat that. They paw the snow off the bunch-grass."

With one big hand, he removed his sombrero with buckskin thongs and fanned himself with it. "If they have to, they'll gnaw on the scrub pine and the cedar. They are as ignorant of corn and oats as they are of Latin. It's a hard life. Passing a winter on the plains is one reason all wild horses are stunted in size. Like that little brown stallion you all talk about."

When it grew too dark to see the hoof marks, they camped. They were careful not to kindle a fire. Wild mustangs can smell smoke for miles.

Next day, they waited until nearly midafternoon for the arrival of Pete Wano's scouts. And old Buck's temper grew as short as his facial foliage tufted long.

"Where in the gol-derned heck are they?" he demanded of Pete Wano. "What's takin' 'em so danged long?"

Wano was patient with the Bar-B owner. "It takes

time, Mr. Boyce, for them to find this wild band," he explained, politely. "It also takes time for them to hide themselves and to hide their odor. Once they get the information they want, it takes time to withdraw quietly. But these are trained men. They'll be here soon."

"Humpf!" snorted old Buck, "how they gonna know where to find us?"

Wano said, "By following the same tracks that we're following—only they'll follow them backwards while we've been following them forwards."

"Humpf!" snorted the old man, and walked off.

At four in the afternoon, the Shoshone scouts came riding through the sage. There were two of them. They were dressed, Dan noticed, about like the Bar-B hands, in Levis, cotton shirts, and California pants. However, they wore rawhide moccasins instead of boots.

Pete Wano went out to meet them. For a moment, they talked. Then Pete Wano came back to Old Buck. Every man pressed closer to hear.

"They have found what we're looking for," he reported. "The wild band, the six steeldust mares, several additional mustangs and mockeys and the brown stallion you call Gaunch."

The younger Shoshone came up to them leading his mount, a dun with zebra stripes down the legs. When he swept off his big Western hat, Dan was surprised to see a boy of about his own age. The Indian youth didn't seem at all abashed to be in the presence of so many rough-looking cowpunchers.

His keen black eyes swept over them briefly but dwelt much longer on their horses, as if determining the value and worth of each. And Dan thought, *I'd hate to have him set out to steal Chico. That is, if I had Chico. He'd probably find a way to do it.*

"The stud is brown, all right, father!" said the boy. "But he also has four white stockings and a white blazed face." To Dan's surprise he spoke in the same

61

correct English as did Pete Wano. His voice had the same musical quality as his father's.

Wano turned to old Buck. "I sent my best scout to locate the band containing your mares'" he said. Gesturing with his head toward the boy, he added, "This is my son Monte."

Dan pressed forward eagerly, facing the younger Wano. "Did you see a grulla pony, mouse-colored, with a black stripe running down his back and legs from his shoulders to his knees?" he asked.

The young Shoshone gave him a straight clear-eyed look. "No, I did not," he said shaking his head. Dan looked inquiringly at the other Shoshone, an older man. That one shook his head, too.

Dan felt a spasm of despair settling in his middle. If Chico wasn't with the wild band, where could he be? Had a mountain lion jumped him? Had he joined another mustang bunch? Was he alive or dead?

"Fergit about that pie eater," growled old Buck. "Time's a wastin'. Les go. Les git as close to 'em as Pete will let us. We gotta build that stockade fence around their water hole."

The Run for Freedom

8

"**I** see 'em!" Dan whispered next morning. "They look like little black specks. They're comin' slow, grazin' while they walk."

He handed the German field glass and its carrying case of worn moroccan leather back to Ben. They were lying side by side in the sage. Other Bar-B cowhands had been stationed at strategic spots in the brush surrounding the small spring that bubbled up invitingly at the foot of the slope.

"That's a good glass," said Dan, continuing to speak softly.

Ben twisted the pearl focusing screw. "Won it at a poker game at Fort Livingston twenty years ago," he whispered.

Below them, built cunningly around the spring and concealed by chopped brush, lay the stockade corral. Its entrance was two hundred yards wide but by the means of long brush fences, or wings, it gradually slanted inwards to the mouth of the trap. It had taken three days to build. The backs and arms of old Buck's Bar-B hands were sore from the unaccustomed labor.

As the wild band came closer, moving towards the precious water they expected to be lapping thirstily, Dan and Ben passed the field glass back and forth. Dan was struck with the rich variety of their colors. There were bays, sorrels, blacks, grays, roans and an occasional paint or buckskin. But no matter how hard Dan looked, he did not see a single grulla.

As they came closer, moving wild and free down the mountain slope, Dan noticed one thing about them that set them apart from ranch horses. These animals loved their liberty.

To know this, Dan had only to watch Gaunch, the brown stallion. When the band grazed, Gaunch climbed a ridge, or stood off to one side by himself. Between bites, he would throw up his head as high as his neck would reach, scrutinizing the landscape or sniffing nervously all around for scents of lurking danger.

They were proud, playful, free-spirited creatures. Most of them, Dan knew, had never known a human master, nor mouthed a bit, nor felt a quirt. They were free to frolic, free to run, free to eat whatever they desired. Freedom was their natural instinct. Dan sensed that they would strive fiercely to maintain it.

On came the wild ones, closer and closer. Their thick manes fell in the wildest disorder across their necks and faces. Their long tails brushed the grass.

And now, in Ben's glass, Dan again saw Gaunch. The little brown stallion had left the ridge and was pacing along the front of the group. His uneasy eye swept the horizon all around.

Dan lowered the glass. Pete Wano's son had been right. There were indeed small white stockings above each of the stallion's feet and a smear of white across his nose.

Dan pulled a long breath, feeling a wave of excitement. This was the tyrant who had stolen Chico and the mares, had nearly killed the quarter horse stallion and had paralyzed the Bar-B's whole operation, plunging it into disorder and confusion.

Dan never knew what set them off. Whatever it was, it came too soon for Pete Wano's careful planning. The brown stallion either caught the odor of the concealed men or distrusted the changed surface features of the trees and brush around the spring.

His screaming whinny split the morning silence. His followers lifted their heads from the bunch grass. For a moment they froze, staring, sniffing, all their heads slanted in the same direction. Then the stallion leaped into action. Neighing shrilly and nipping flanks, he rushed them into swiftly flowing motion.

Acting quickly in the crisis, the two Shoshones broke from their hiding spots behind the wild band. Yelling loudly, they started them on a terrified run for the hidden corral.

Earl Stains, wearing his goatskin chaps, darted out from behind a tree and joined the pursuit. He was shouting and lashing his horse with his reins. Others of old Buck's group appeared as suddenly as from the earth itself and joined the chase.

Dan's heart gave a leap. The project was succeeding wonderfully well. The wild ones were being forced at high speed between the wing fences and straight toward the stockade trap. Their hoofbeats came back to Dan like the roll of drums.

Riding Rollie at a dead run on the outer limits, Dan felt himself a part of the exciting spectacle. The fleeing animals all bore a wild, startled look. Snorting loudly, they crashed through the sage. The brush was crackling and popping. The dust beneath their hooves rose in a cloud.

To Dan's surprise, the steeldust mares had taken upon themselves all the mannerisms of the wild ones. Nostrils distended, manes erect, tails strung out behind them in a straight line, they acted as if they were running for their lives, too. They seemed entirely different from their former civilized selves.

The brown stallion, circling to the rear where the

enemy was first revealed, did not panic. He ran easily and relaxed, his feet clicking on the rocks. As he skimmed along close to the ground, he looked back coolly and disdainfully at his pursuers as if to say, I know what I can do, and I know what you can do, too. I'm not going to waste my best speed until the occasion demands it.

And then suddenly the occasion did demand it. The brown stallion, raising his head suspiciously as he ran, seemed to smell danger ahead. Neighing shrilly, he spurted, sweeping past his entire band, drawing them away from the trap. Then he cut to the right, taking a direction away from the corral.

But Pete Wano's coyote dun, with the big Shoshone's heels thumping against his rib cage, ran with the pitiless speed of a panicked antelope. He dashed squarely across the stallion's path.

Wano, shaking out one end of his rawhide rope, began beating the stallion across the nose with its knotted end. He had to turn him back toward the trap corral. The wild band would follow the stud blindly wherever he went.

The brown stud reared up and struck at Wano's mount with his front feet. His eyes, thrust out from their sockets, blazed fiery red with hate. With his mouth opened wide like a wolf's and his lips rolled back, exposing his teeth, he tried to bite the coyote dun, an expression of murder in his eyes.

The dun dodged, its ears drawn back to avoid being bitten. And Wano kept shouting and swinging his rope as a whip.

It was then that the encounter took on an entirely different phase. With the wild herd slowed, the animals rearing in confusion and the stallion momentarily halted and occupied, a new leader assumed command.

A chestnut mare, acting coolly in the crisis, made a sudden shy to the left, away from the corral, and dashed straight toward the opposite wing fence. The wild ones followed her with complete confidence. The brush fence looming, she leaped entirely over it, dislodging part of it with one hip and widening the opening for those following. One by one, the wild ones streamed through it.

Then Dan, staring wide eyed, saw that she wore a halter. Ben Dragoo, riding alongside, noticed it too.

"That's Jewel!" he cried, an expression of stunned disbelief in his eyes. "We've got to stop her!" Slapping his bay with his reins, he tried to catch her. But he tried in vain.

Old Buck, astride what he thought was the fastest horse on the ranch, a roan with bay ears and white mane and tail, joined the pursuit. Dan was surprised at how well his great-uncle sat his horse. The old man stuck to his mount like a burr to a saddle blanket.

For a moment, he was closer to the mare than anybody. His face was strained with astonishment when he saw his former pet, his darling. He knew that she could hear him.

"Jewel! Jewel!" he shouted to her in his broken, far carrying voice. "Come girl! Come girl! Come with me!"

But she didn't come. She didn't seem to want to. She was flying. And the wild band, steeldusts and all, flew with her. And Dan, Ben, and old Buck fell farther and farther behind. Their mounts were carrying riders and had not the incentive of the mustangs.

A volley of hooves rang out behind them. The sound came closer. Then the brown stallion swept past Dan, and Ben, and old Buck, and took his place at the rear of the mustang express. There he could watch things and keep the stragglers moving. He seemed to have perfect trust in his chestnut pace setter to lead the band wisely and well.

As Jewel joyously led the run for freedom, Dan

grudgingly had to give her credit. She's got wonderful speed, he told himself.

Her first object seemed to be to put distance between the wild ones and the Bar-B riders. That done, she showed that she knew the area like she'd known her stall in the old man's barn.

Turning in a long shallow arc, she sped toward the foothills, where there were timber, boulders, and canyons. And Dan knew that this was a place where saddle horses with riders could not go.

"Look at her!" panted Ben, riding on Dan's right. "Now she's scattering 'em in the brush! They'll each go their own separate way, like so many quail."

A stunned look on his face, old Buck watched her out of sight. "Dang it, she's gone, too!" he whispered, wringing his hands. "All my beautiful mares is gone!"

When he rode back to join them, his roan was blowing in deep gasping sobs. As old Buck's foreman, Ben Dragoo knew better than anybody the closeness that had existed between Jewel and the old man.

"She didn't hear you, Mr. Boyce," said Ben, loyally.

"Yes she did!" burst out the old man bitterly. "She heared me, all right! She knowed me! There's nothin' wrong with her eyes, her ears, her nose or her memory. She jist didn't wanta stop."

Ben said, "If she ever got near the ranch, I bet she'd come in."

Old Buck's whiskery face was strained with anger. He beat his left fist into his right palm.

"Naw!" he panted, crossly. "She's as wild as that brown stud. In fact, she's wilder than him. An' as good a leader, too."

He beat his right fist into his left palm. "Gol dang it!" he moaned. "What got into her? Now we gotta do it all over again."

Dan felt sorry for the old fellow. He knew exactly how his great-uncle felt, having himself lost Chico to the wild ones.

"Well, Uncle Buck, at least you got to see her," he said. "You oughta be glad she's alive. Everybody's been sayin' she's dead."

"Humpf!" snorted the old man. "She's worse than dead. She's joined the broomtails an' the fuzzies."

He jerked his hat down over his eyes and waited for the roan to get its breath.

Ben Dragoo spat in the sage. "I was surprised to see how skinny she looked. But it's helped her speed. I never saw her run so fast, or hold her speed so well."

Old Buck glared at him. "She always could run fast an' fur," he said. "She always was as speedy a one as ever looked through a bridle."

Or a halter, thought Dan. But he didn't say so. He didn't want to add to the old man's woes.

Pete Wano rode up on his coyote dun. He was recoiling his long rawhide reata.

"I'm sorry, Mr. Boyce," he said. "That smart little stud stampeded them a few seconds too soon." He switched the coiled loop to the opposite side of his saddle. "They tell me that the mare you lost years ago was the leader of the wild ones today. They change, don't they?"

Old Buck's eyes gleamed with anger and hurt. "They shore do," he said, brokenly. "They shore as dang heck do."

Pete Wano swept off his big hat and fanned himself with it. "We've got a little good news for you," he said. "They roped one of your steeldust mares. We didn't get blanked."

Ben said, "Them steeldusts ran faster today than any of our ranch hosses. Wonder what got into 'em?"

Wano tied his looped reata to his saddle. "The call of the wild comes to the gentlest of horses when they are thrown with wild ones that have grown up free of all restraint," he said. "They think they're supposed to run as fast as the wild ones. And sometimes they do."

Old Buck took off his hat and sleeved the sweat off his shiny dome. "When can we start after 'em again?"

"Next spring," replied Wano. The old man looked disappointed.

"An' what do we use next time?"

"About the same thing we did this time except we'll have a canvas corral with canvas wings that they can't break through," said Wano.

"Canvas? Why didn't we use canvas this time?" Old Buck wanted to know. Dan, on Rollie, wanted to ask the same question.

"Because there wasn't time," said Pete Wano. "You were in a hurry. And the stockade method sometimes works. If we change to canvas, we'll have to haul the canvas corral and wings sixty miles by pack train. That takes time. But once we get it to the water hole we can set it up in two hours.

"I know a young ranchman who gets his mail at Elko. He captures hundreds of wild horses every year, using canvas fences and corrals."

Ben said, "But there's no strength in canvas, is there?"

Wano looked at him and nodded. "That's right. But the wild horses don't know that. They never try to jump anything they can't see through or over. These canvas fences begin a foot above the ground and stand seven or eight feet high. To the wild ones, they look like a rock wall. They don't try to break them down."

"Sixty miles is a long way to haul that much canvas, ain't it?" Earl Stains asked.

Wano said, "It's so light that it can be packed in sections on the backs of pack animals. They can carry it easily to the roughest part of the mountains. Once you find the spot, the whole thing can be set up in two hours. It just takes time to haul it to where your scouts find the horses and their water hole."

Old Buck rode the roan back to where the lone steeldust mare was calmly grazing, staked out by a rope.

"Humpf!" he grunted, in disgust. "She's the only one of the bunch I didn't like."

Monte Wano

After supper in the mess hall the next night, several of the Bar-B cowboys lingered to discuss the unsuccessful hunt. Dan was among them.

Nobody noticed him. Head down, he was devouring Carmen's hot biscuits and beef. After six days chasing wild horses, he was very hungry.

Jack Boyd, a big fellow with eyes like a fish, was talking. He had just joined the outfit, replacing Dave Gleason who had broken an ankle in a corral accident.

"Did you hear what he said about us all goin' on another of them wild hoss hunts in the spring?" Boyd asked. His voice was raspy with anger. "This time we're gonna string canvas fences all over north-central Nevada."

"Yeah," chimed in somebody else, "but they gotta have cedar posts to string 'em to. That means more choppin' an' diggin'."

With the back of his hand, Jack Boyd pushed his plate roughly across the table. It clattered noisily against the cups and saucers.

"I didn't hire on here as no wood chopper," he said. "I ride, an' rope, an' brand, an' bust broncs. I don't like bein' asked to do somethin' on foot. Why don't he watch his mares better? If he spent half as much time watchin' 'em as he does pettin' 'em, they'd all be here today."

Dan stiffened and felt his breathing quicken. He raised his head from his plate. For the first time, he realized they were talking about his great-uncle.

"What's wrong with pettin' a horse if you like him?" he asked mildly. As always, his thoughts were on the absent Chico.

The others looked at him in surprise. Boyd swung his cold fish eyes full upon him. "Nothin', I guess," he said. "But if I had six expensive mares an' really liked 'em, I wouldn't turn 'em loose on the range."

Dan winced. He didn't like this bad mouthing the boss. They were all grown men, but he decided to stand up to them.

Dan said, "He had a man—Tex Tolbert—watchin' them. He was just switchin' them from one range to another."

"What you gettin' so ring-tailed about, kid?" spoke up George Claxton, roughly. "What's the old man ever done fer you?"

Dan laid down his knife and fork and sat up straight. "First of all, he's my own blood and kin," he said. "That means something to me."

Claxton sneered. "It must not mean much to him or he'd have you stayin' with him in the big white house."

Dan looked at him coolly. "What's wrong with livin' in the bunkhouse?" he asked. "I like livin' in it." He knew that he had them there. They all lived in the bunkhouse, too.

Claxton turned to Boyd. "This kid is the old man's great-nephew," he said. "Name of Dan Deweese."

Boyd's mouth went flat from shock. He said no more. *He's afraid I'll tattle on him to Uncle Buck*, Dan thought as he buttered a biscuit triumphantly.

73

But George Claxton wasn't so cautious. "You didn't answer my question, kid," he said. "What's he ever done fer you?"

Dan looked at him with irritation. The man was mixing in something that was none of his business.

"Plenty," he replied. "He took me in. He gave me a job. He fed me. He put me up. I'm learnin' cowboyin' on his ranch. He pays me twenty dollars a month. He's sendin' me to school." He hadn't realized before the extent of his debt to his great-uncle.

He thought of his stepdad back in Nebraska and wanted to add, "And he doesn't steal it from me, either. Or sell my horse." But he didn't. That was his own personal affair.

With a jingle of spurs and a sliding of boots on the floor, Claxton and Boyd got up and went out.

Still upset at their lack of loyalty, Dan poured honey on his biscuit and over his thumb, too. Then he popped both into his mouth. Even if his great-uncle was grumpy, he was lots better off here on the Bar-B than he'd be at home, and he knew it.

Only one thing bothers me, he told himself. If I could just find Chico . . . .

Next afternoon Monte Wano, the son of mustanger Pete, came by on his dun with the zebra stripes down the legs. Dan was at the woodpile.

Dan stood, holding the axe in both hands. "Hello," he said.

"I saw your horse yesterday," said Monte Wano, coming straight to the point as was his custom.

"Where?" blurted Dan. Blinking with excitement, he leaned his axe against the fresh-cut pile.

Monte Wano gestured with his head toward the northern foothills. It was the same gesture his father used, Dan remembered.

"Up there," he answered unsmilingly, "near the down slash. It would be easier to take you there than to try to tell you."

"Let's go now," said Dan, eagerly.

Monte Wano said, "I tried to catch him for you. I saw him coming. With the wind blowing from him to me I was able to hide my horse behind a big boulder without his smelling me. I shot my rope at him. But he dodged my loop and ran off from my horse here."

Reaching down, he patted the shoulders of the dun. "I didn't think any horse could do that. But that little grulla did. He got so far ahead so fast that we both got discouraged trying to follow him."

Dan felt a happy humming in his head. "That's Chico, all right," he burst out. "How did he look?"

"Pretty wild," said Monte Wano. "His forelock was full of cockleburrs. You may have to rope him."

"I don't think so," said Dan. "I think he's like your father's coyote dun. He follows me everywhere, just like the dun follows your father. I think he knows me so well that if he saw me, or heard me whistle, he'd come to me. Like he always did."

"Roping is the best way," the young Shoshone insisted. "My father roped the only steeldust mare that didn't get away on this last hunt. He had to throw a long rope to get her. But he got her."

Dan looked down at his boots and shook his head. "I don't rope very well yet," he said, ashamed of it. "I'm improving, but that's all. José is the best roper on the Bar-B."

For a moment there was silence between them.

"Your horse will never go lame on you," said Monte Wano in another of his deep pronouncements.

Puzzled, Dan raised his head in surprise. "How do you know that?" he asked.

"Because he's got black hooves," said Monte Wano.

"That's right, he has," said Dan. "But what difference does that make?"

Monte Wano explained. "Wild horses wear no shoes. So the color of the hoof is much regarded. The

75

yellow hoof with white hair is brittle. It soon wears away and grows sore. Black hooves are best."

Thinking of Chico, and his ebony underpinning, Dan felt proud. He hadn't known.

"A grulla's hooves are like flint," the Shoshone went on. "The rocky country keeps them sharp. My father says that in the old days the Shoshones took only black-hoofed horses on their war expeditions."

He shooed a fly off his horse's ear. "Is he gelded?" he asked.

Dan nodded. "When he was eighteen months old."

Dan pulled his gloves on tighter. "I'd better ask my great-uncle if I can go with you," he said. "Want to come in with me?" Monte Wano slid off his horse and left the reins dangling.

They found old Buck bent over his ledgers in the sitting room. He was smoking his French brier pipe with a heavy nickel band on the stem.

Dan pointed at Monte Wano. "Uncle Buck, he saw my horse yesterday. He almost roped him. He says he can lead me to him. Can I go?"

The old man scowled. "Naw!" he said, curtly. "He's full grown now. Tryin' to catch a full-grown broomtail is like tryin' to catch a sunbeam in a basket. Fergit him." He turned back to his ledgers.

Monte Wano stood proudly in the background as if he did not like being ignored. His chin rose. "I talked to my father about it," he said. "My father says the wild ones feed lower down in the fall. He thinks we might catch this one."

Old Buck whirled around. He glared at Monte Wano. "What does your father know about it?" he growled. "Who in the gol darn heck is your father?"

Dan broke in, "Uncle Buck, his father is Pete Wano, the mustanger. This is Monte Wano, his son. Don't you remember him? He and the other Shoshone scout found the water hole of the brown stallion and his band, remember?"

Old Buck took his pipe out of his mouth. He stared with more respect at Monte Wano. But the Indian boy, still wearing his proud look, stared only at the distant wall.

Old Buck glared at Dan. "Why didn't you say it was him in the first place?" he growled. And Dan thought, *now he's saying it's my fault that he didn't recognize Monte. Nothing's ever his fault.*

Again Monte Wano lifted his chin. Speaking in his slow, thoughtful manner, he said, "We might see the brown stallion and his band on this trip. It might be useful to know if they still range in this locality. And how many of your mares are still with him."

Dan's opinion of Monte Wano soared sky high. Dan thought that Monte had said exactly the right thing to get Uncle Buck's interest and attention. It was the one thing he could have said that might get them on their way looking for Chico.

Then the Indian lad scored again. "My father thinks we are sure to get the steeldust mares for you next summer—those of them that are still living. He has already arranged to rent the canvas corral and the wings of cloth and bunting."

Wildly excited, old Buck found his voice. "Who's he rentin' 'em from?" he demanded.

"From Charley Barnum," Monte Wano replied. "He owns a ranch near ours. I go to school at Elko with his son and daughter."

"Gol dern!" the old man snorted gleefully. "I wish we could start tomorry."

He turned to Dan, frowning. "How many days would you be gone lookin' fer yore broomtail?"

Dan looked inquiringly at Monte Wano. "How many?"

"Not many," replied the mustanger's son, "I saw him yesterday morning while hunting antelope. We can go to that spot in a day, now that I know where he is. He shouldn't be too far away. Unless he's been spooked. Then we could still follow his tracks."

"I don't think you'll catch him," said old Buck, "but go ahead and try. Tell Tonia and Ben I said to put you up some food an' beddin'. Better take several canteens of water. Hosses might get thusty afore you git back. Water is scarce up there. Water 'em real good afore you leave. Keep yore eyes peeled for my mares. Tell me what you see."

Before they rode out, Dan found Ben and told him where they were going.

"Wait," said Ben. "Walk with me down past my house. I want to loan you my field glass. Might come in handy."

The Piñon Tree

Monte led off on his zebra-striped dun, heading straight toward the distant foothills. Dan followed, riding Freddie and leading Rollie, on whose back the supplies were packed.

It was late in August and still hot. The grass had begun to wither and brown. Fallen aspen leaves were piling along the dry ravines. Sweat ran down the flanks of the horses and made queer little smudges in the powdered dust below.

In midafternoon they made their only rest stop. It contrasted the relaxing habits of the white boy and the Shoshone. Dan sprawled on his back in the shade of a creosote bush, his hat tilted to protect his eyes from the sun. Monte crouched in the way his forefathers had crouched for generations, squatting on his moccasin heels in a fashion that permitted the smallest possible exposure to the sun, yet eased the muscles strained by the saddle.

Cinches were loosened. Bits were taken from mouths so that the horses could graze easier. Dan pulled off a boot to smooth a wrinkle in his sock.

Monte Wano said, abruptly, "I talked to my father about you and your grulla."

This time Dan was not surprised. "What did he say?" asked Dan.

"He said if you ever get your pony back to the ranch he will probably stay with you this time," Monte Wano replied. "He says that you can't fool a horse. A horse knows whether or not you like him."

Dan gave a long gasping sigh. "I sure like him," he said, "and I know he likes me, too. But I worry that he may have got spooky and shy while we've been separated. Now that he's had a taste of the wild, I'm afraid he might want to live there always, like his ancestors."

"Maybe not," said Monte, poking in the sand with a stick. "I think we'll find his little band tomorrow. Then we'll find out where they go for water. It's hot. They have to drink someplace."

That night, Dan hobbled Freddie and Rollie, buckling a strap around a front and rear leg on the same side of each. Monte turned the zebra-legged dun loose with no tether.

"He won't run off," he said. He seemed very sure.

Excited at being so close to his lost pony, Dan ate but little, and that standing up. He was too nervous to strike a more restful pose. He slept poorly, too. He awakened twice in the middle of the night, and sat up, listening. But all he heard was the hooting of an owl.

Next morning, an hour after they resumed the hunt, they found what they were after.

"There they are," whispered Monte, handing Ben's binoculars back to Dan. "Dab the glass on them. I know it's the same bunch because there's a white and a black grazing together. Just like day before yesterday."

With much twisting of the pearl focusing screw, Dan saw them browsing down the side of a hill less than a mile away.

"I see him!" muttered Dan as he picked out Chico in the glass. The grulla was grazing in a scanty copse of sage brush and shad scale. For a moment Dan breathed faster and felt the goose pimples rising on his forearms. It felt great to see his horse again, even a mile away through a glass. It was good to know that he was alive.

"I can tell it's him by his gait," exulted Dan. "He grazes at a faster walk than the others. Wonder why they aren't with the brown stallion's band?"

"He probably drove them off," said Monte Wano. "A stud prefers only mares. But he'll usually put up with their colts and once in a while with mules and saddle horses."

Dan lowered the glass. "This is rough country," he said, looking around. "Lots of timber and hills and rocks. How're we going to find their watering hole?"

"Now that we've found them, I know where it is already," said Monte. "There's only one around here and it isn't far. Pretty soon they'll get thirsty and take us to it."

That's exactly what happened. At the bottom of a deep gorge that wasn't visible until they came upon it suddenly, they found the watering place of the band. The big gash seemed to drop off directly under Freddie's nose.

At first, its walls looked far too steep for any horse to descend. The cliffs, on one of which Dan and Monte Wano stood, were craggy and rough. Their faces were mostly sheer rock without bushes or small tree growth for handholds. Chamise, chaparral, and sage grew in tangles among the boulders.

But down on the canyon's floor lay a green glade. There wildflowers grew and butterflies floated lazily. Dan knew that this small meadow had to be freshened by a spring. This had to be where the mustangs did their drinking.

By careful use of Ben's glass, the boys saw the small band enter and leave the canyon. A single such trip took almost a full hour. They usually drank at night.

Dan frowned. "There's got to be a trail here someplace so they can get in and out of that big thing to drink," he said. Monte nodded soberly.

They found it next morning and were pleased with the opportunity it gave for the success of their undertaking. The trail entered the canyon at a spot where the horses had to walk in single file, hooves sliding, heads held low, between high banks and several huge boulders.

"We'd better stay away from that trail," warned Monte, "or our scent will frighten them. My father says more wild horses are lost through scenting those hunting them than by any other way."

Even if Chico smelled me, it would be a familiar smell and he might not panic, thought Dan.

They came to the place where the trail left the rim and began twisting downward into the gorge. Just over this spot grew a tall piñon tree nearly forty feet in height.

It was Monte who suggested a bold plan. "Why don't you climb the tree and hang your rope from its lower branches?" he proposed. "The moon will be shining brightly. You could lower the rope with the noose fixed in such a way that you could drop it over his head when he walked under it on his way down. He can't smell you so good if you're high."

Dan frowned. "What if my rope missed?" he said. "He probably wouldn't stop running until he got clear to California."

Monte said, "If you missed him here, I might rope him as he came through the narrow opening at the other end of the gorge. There are some cedars there I could hide behind."

They decided to try it that way. The plan was chancy but it was the best they could think of. They had no stockade trap nor canvas corral. There were only two of them instead of fifteen or twenty.

Just before dark, Dan climbed the tree. He was careful to scale its back side, away from the trail, to lessen his scent. He carefully laid out his noose, dangling it from the piñon's branches just above the trail. He took care to hold it high enough to clear a horse's head.

The other end he wrapped around a branch in the tree's middle boughs. He settled himself on a limb and raised a hand to Monte as the young Shoshone started his ride around the canyon to the trail's other end.

Perched in the limbs of the piñon, Dan waited. But no horses came. The moon arose from the east and swung across the heavens. Still no horses. Twice Dan dozed off. The muscles of his legs and hips became so cramped that he was tempted to climb down to ease them. Then he thought of Chico, and how badly he wanted him back. He decided to tough it out, staying on his roost.

Just as the stars began to fade, he heard the snort of a horse and the hollow clatter of hooves on rocks. Then came a steady tramping of feet and the sound of small pebbles kicked loose and rolling. Dan was now wide awake. He fingered his rope and felt his breath snagging in his throat.

The first horse passing beneath the piñon was the milk white. It was easily seen in the moonlight. Dan shivered in excitement. Then came the jet black, a dark blur against a light background. He was harder to see, but recognizable.

And then came Chico.

Dan was certain it was he. The pony's mouse-gray color was indistinct in the moonlight. But Dan had no trouble identifying the smallish, neat body or the quick clear-footed gait.

Just as Chico walked beneath the dangling noose, Dan dropped the loop over his head. The pony sprang forward with a snort of terror. Dan bared his teeth and breathed in deeply.

"I've got him!" he told himself, joyfully.

And then he didn't have him. In all their planning, Dan and Monte had not thought of one thing, the tremendous backlash of the tree limb.

Clutching the rope in both hands, Dan leaned far over, the better to see the horse below. This left him off balance. When the seven hundred-pound weight of the frightened pony reached the end of the rope, the tree was bent far forward.

Plunging against the suddenly tightened rope, Chico was jerked off balance and fell. That ripped the rope out of Dan's hands. The snap and spring of the big tree backward to its erect position sent the boy flying from his perch like a stone from a slingshot. He landed in a clump of cedar, several feet away.

When Dan regained his senses, it was broad daylight. He was lying on his back on the ground. He felt a gentle nudge in his ribs. Something was blowing its hot breath in his face.

Then he heard the chomping of teeth on grass. He shut his eyes in contentment. He was very tired.

Presently he opened his eyes again and was overjoyed to see Chico grazing, a step at a time, nearby.

"Hey, Chico," Dan called, weakly.

At the sound of the boy's voice, the grulla raised his head and nickered softly. Then he resumed feeding.

He knows me, Dan thought happily. Chico still had Dan's rope around his neck, but the end of it was dragging free on the ground.

Dan sat up. His head ached and he felt sore and bruised all over. His face was scratched, his hands blistered. His clothing was torn and rumpled. He rolled to his knees and stayed there a minute until the dizziness passed. Then he climbed slowly to his feet.

Chico came up to him. Whinnying softly, he nosed Dan all over, as if inquiring about his health and welfare. Dan patted the horse's neck and squeezed his ears. The grulla yawned contentedly.

With one hand, Dan felt of the cockleburrs enmeshed in Chico's forelocks that fell like flaxen bangs down past his eyes.

"You're shaggy as a buffalo," Dan said. "Wait til I get you back to the Bar-B, my friend. My curry comb's gonna get a good workout."

Then the boy remembered. "You still haven't had a drink, have you?" he said. "You let the rest of your band go fill up with water while you stayed here with me." Dan was thrilled by the wonder of it. No need to worry anymore about his pet running off to join the wild ones.

He found his hat and filled it half full of water from his canteen. He had hidden the canteen in a chaparral bush behind the hill. Chico guzzled the water eagerly, every last drop of it. Then Dan led him down the canyon trail to the green meadow. They both took a long drink in the spring.

Later they found Monte Wano at the far end of the trail at the canyon's exit. The Shoshone, looking very sleepy, still held his rope in his hand. Dan told him what had happened.

"He was loose and could have run away," said Dan proudly. "But he didn't. He heard my voice. He smelled me. And I reckon he smelled my rope, too. He stayed."

After they had breakfasted on the last of Tonia's food, Dan thanked Monte Wano warmly for all his help. Raising his hand, Monte, on the zebra dun, headed north toward his father's ranch.

Dan cut straight across the foothills to the Bar-B. When they drew near the outbuildings, Dan felt a quickening of the heart, a growing eagerness of one coming home after an absence that seemed long. How well he had come to like the Bar-B, the sprawl of its log buildings, the sweep of its bunch grass range, the smell of its sun-heated sage.

Riding Chico and leading Freddie and Rollie, he was the proudest cowboy who ever straddled a horse.

The Red Sweater

Upon their return, Chico behaved almost as if he'd never been gone. Mischief was still his dish and he feasted from it often.

Impatient with fences and gates, he became more clever than ever breaching them so that he could follow Dan about the grounds. Just to be forever with Dan seemed his dearest wish.

One morning when Dan was carrying a cedar pail of milk to Carmen's kitchen, he saw Tonia come out the back door with a sprinkler. She was going to water her flowers.

Her gasp of surprise and dismay brought Dan quickly to her side.

"Oh!" she moaned softly. "My poor delphiniums! Look at them!"

Dan tried to look but there was nothing to see. Chico's footprints were everywhere. Jumping the fence, the mustang had eaten both rows of the delicate blossoms and also their feathery leaves. Blue petals lay scattered about the soft earth.

"I'm awful sorry, Tonia," Dan apologized. "I'll help you replant them." And he did. Moreover, he built a wire mesh over them.

To himself, he said: When's my pony going to

stop behaving like an impish child? When's he going to grow up?

Two days later Ben Dragoo's sister, a music teacher from Wyoming, was visiting at Ben's home. Dan was invited for supper. Afterwards, Ben took her to the big house to meet old Buck.

"Come on in an' sit," old Buck invited. Dan wasn't at all sure the invitation included him. With Ben pushing him from behind, he had to follow the women into the sitting room.

The guest's eye fell upon the parlor organ of solid oak that the old man had long ago purchased for his wife. Since her death, it had sat untouched in a corner of the sitting room. A fringed scarf of silk was draped over it.

Ben's sister caught her breath when she saw it. Smiling and eager, she looked at old Buck.

"What a beautiful instrument," she said, running her hand along its carved face. "May I play it?" She didn't know that it hadn't been played for years.

Mistaking old Buck's confused silence for consent, she seated herself at the instrument. She began exploring the keyboard, pumping the foot pedals and pulling the celluloid stops. Then she began to play.

The mellow notes of "Amazing Grace," the old Baptist religious hymn, filled the room melodiously. Pleased, Dan raised his head and felt his breathing quicken.

"What a wonderful tone it has," the woman praised. Other tunes of the time twinkled off her fingers. Among them were "Long Long Ago," "Old Black Joe," "Red River Valley" and "The Girl I Loved in Sunny Tennessee."

In the midst of "Annie Laurie" old Buck got up quietly. Without a word, he walked from the room.

Dan thought, he's saddened because the song reminds him of his wife. Her name was Annie, too. The boy wished that he might have seen and known his great-aunt. If just the memory of her could move a crusty character like old Buck, she must have been a very lovable lady.

Next morning it was raining softly. After Dan finished milking, he took the grulla into the barn to groom him. From the big house, Tonia called.

"*Señor* Dan, can you please come and help me move the furniture?" she asked. "I want to sweep and mop the floors in Mr. Boyce's room."

When Dan returned to the barn, Chico wasn't in the stall where he had left him. Instead, he found the pony in the barn's runway. Chico was eating something hanging from the back of the old man's saddle which hung from a peg on the wall.

Hearing Dan's approach, Chico looked around at him. From the pony's lips, Dan saw a strand of red thread dangling.

Dan gasped and felt his mouth go dry. Running to the horse, he saw that Chico had eaten one arm off the old man's beloved red sweater. He had eaten it off clear up to the shoulder. The last of the elastic cuff was going down the mustang's throat.

"No no, Chico!" Dan yelled, yanking the sweater out of the grulla's mouth.

Holding it up, he looked at it with dismay. He shook his head, dreading to break the news to the garment's owner. But somebody had to.

When Dan told the old man about it, old Buck's face went hard as flint. His blue eyes held an almost feverish shine.

"Now lissen to me, boy!" he said. "I want you to take that gol-derned fuzz-tail clean off this ranch and never bring him back. Git rid of him! Do it right this minute! You can stay if you want to but he can't. He's through! He's no good." He flung what was left of the sweater on the ground. Muttering to himself, he walked off.

Dan felt his own temper rising. He went to the bunkhouse and began to pack his things.

"Where you goin'?" came Ben Dragoo's calm voice from behind him.

Dan looked up, a pair of folded jeans in his hands. He told Ben what had happened.

Ben spat coolly out the open door into a mud puddle. A little silver geyser leaped upward from where the spittle struck. "Yore not goin' anywheres an' neither is yore hoss," he said.

Dan stood. Creasing his hat, he put it on. He liked the red-haired foreman but he'd made up his mind. He picked up his bed roll.

"Dan, when you gonna learn how to handle yore great-uncle?" Ben went on. "Sit down a minute. I'll tell you what we'll do."

Dan sat down. But he kept his hat on.

"Ain't you gonna take off yore hat?" Ben asked, good humoredly.

"No sir!" said Dan. "I want it on. So if he insults me again about my horse, I'll be ready to leave right off."

Ben said, "Mr. Boyce is short tempered and impatient and says things he don't mean at all three or four days later. Turn Chico into the feed lot an' wire both gates shut. Watch him careful. If you can keep him out of Mr. Boyce's sight until tomorrow mornin' I think he'll forget all about what he said."

"How's that going to help?" Dan wanted to know. "Tomorrow morning comes pretty quick."

"I'll tell you how," said Ben. "Stains an' Tolbert and Rawson are drivin' a bunch of calves to the railroad at Elko startin' in the mornin'. I'm hereby assignin' you on Chico—to go along an' help 'em. You'll be gone a week. By that time it'll all blow over."

Dan bit down on his lower lip. His ears still burned. "I like it here," he said, "but if Chico ever leaves the Bar-B, I'm leavin' with him."

Ben spat through the open window into a hedge outside. "Of course you will," he said. "I know how you feel about him. I know how Mr. Boyce feels, too.

He's had that sweater for years an' years. His dead wife gave it to him. It's like an old friend. You've got to learn to look at it from his angle, too."

Dan cooled down and took his hat off. He took the sweater to Tonia.

"Don't worry about it, *señor* Dan," she said. "I have some red yarn. I can knit him another sleeve."

And she did. Three days later, she held it for old Buck to try on.

"Humpf!" the old man snapped gruffly. "Fits purty good. Looks purty good, too." After that, he kept the garment in the blacksmith shop.

And Dan thought, "whatever would I do on this ranch without Ben and Tonia?"

Soon it was late October. There was a lull in the work about the ranch. Preparations were nearly finished for the coming of winter.

The fall roundup was over. The last load of prairie hay was gathered and stacked. The corn had been placed in ricks in the feed lot.

Under Ben's direction, the roofs of the cook shack and the bunkhouse were inspected and the shingles patched. The stovepipes were refitted on one another. On the cellar floor, great barrels of flour, potatoes, and pickled pork were stored. Two smaller barrels held eggs put down in lime. Apple butter, jam, and sweet pickle lay in lard pails nearby.

Dan, on Chico, went with Tex Tolbert and Lee Rawson to drive a bunch of calves to the railroad at Elko. It was the last drive of the year. On the way back, a cloud came up suddenly out of the northwest. Rolling over and over, it looked like a gigantic tumbleweed loose in the wind.

As it folded continually on itself, its color changed from white to green to black. Dan drew on his gloves. He took his rolled yellow slicker from behind the cantle of his saddle and put it on.

The wind began to blow out of the north, whipping the bunch grass. Big flakes of popcorn-sized snow began to fall. Soon the sky was so filled with it that little could be seen of the surrounding country. All vision died at fifteen feet.

"Where are we?" Tolbert yelled.

"About ten miles from the ranch, I think," Rawson replied.

"Yeah, but where's the ranch?" Tolbert asked.

"I don't know," said Rawson. "I can't see. There's no fence to guide us. We've lost the trail."

Dan said, "We'd better stay close together or we might get lost from each other."

They were huddled low in their saddles, Dan bringing up the rear. Jacket collars were turned up. Hat brims were held down by bandanna neckerchiefs bound tightly over the crown and tied underneath their chins.

Dan's feet felt numb in the stirrups. When he breathed with his mouth open, the cold felt like a stab in his chest. Occasionally they got off to walk, their gloved hands slapping their legs to the rhythm of their horses' hooves. That warmed their feet, but could they walk all night?

"Reckon we oughta hole up someplace an' try to camp?" asked Rawson.

"Naw!" said Tolbert. "We ain't got no campin' gear. We ain't got no way to git outta this wind, either. The country's too flat."

Rawson said, "If we could set a match to one of these sage bushes, we'd shore have us a bright fire. Somebody might see us."

They stopped and tried it. As fast as Rawson snapped a sulphur match the wind blew out the flame. After he tried it twenty times, they got back on their horses and continued riding.

Now Chico, head down, was leading, striding along like a machine. The other two horses followed, looking very tired. Occasionally they lagged back so far that Tolbert and Rawson had to lash them and scold them sharply.

Twice Dan dozed in the saddle. Each time he roused himself. We're still drifting aimlessly, he told himself. We're lost.

Suddenly, from out of the swirling snow ahead, the top rails of a wooden fence rose out of the gloom. There was the faint odor of a barn. Chico stuck his head over the plank gate and stopped. He looked around at Dan as if to say, this is as far as I can go. Now it's your job to open this thing and take us in where it's warm.

"Holy Hop Toads!" Tolbert yelled joyfully. "We're home and didn't know it!"

"That little mouse-colored devil knew it!" Rawson said. "He knew it all along. He must be carrying a compass between his eyes."

Dan felt a choking lump of pride in his throat. He got off and hugged his pony's neck. He opened the gate and led Chico into the barn. Tolbert and Rawson followed.

As he poured oats from the bin into Chico's feed box, Dan remembered what Ben Dragoo had once told him, "Some of the best horses I ever owned was the wild ones I broke myself. They had a great sense of smell. They knew where they was goin' and what they was doin' every minute.

"Give 'em a loose rein," Ben had said. "Let them do the runnin' and the choosing'."

Dan rubbed Chico's nearest ear and laughed. "You did a good job of choosing tonight, chum," he told the mustang. "And you did it all by yourself."

The second hunt for the brown stallion's band again became a test of patience.

Most impatient of all was old Buck himself. He had been wanting to start the expedition since early spring.

"As I've explained to Mr. Boyce, we can't get in a hurry about this," Pete Wano told the Bar-B hands during dinner in the cook shack. He had arrived early in July to take charge.

His brown eyes, keen slits hooded by heavy brows, swept over them.

"We can't rush things," he went on. "The wild ones won't come down out of the mountains until they've given up searching for the scattered snow patches. When these are all melted, they won't have anything to drink. Then they'll have to come down to the springs in the foothills. And we'll be ready for them."

To his great delight, Dan was permitted to accompany Monte Wano to scout the movements of the wild band. This time the pony Freddie went along as a pack horse.

When the two boys rode by the house to borrow Ben's field glass, Pete Wano's keen eyes became fixed on Chico. Head up, the grulla was stepping along in his quick, perky way, watchfully surveying everything around him.

"Whose horse is that?" Pete Wano asked.

"He's jist a pesky little fuzz-tail," muttered old Buck. "Belongs to my grand-nephew," he added, wiping his runny nose across the sleeve of his flannel shirt.

The big mustanger kept looking at Chico. "Hmm," he murmured, "I like the way he moves." Monte Wano, who had lingered to speak to his father, told Dan about the incident later.

"Better hobble that broomtail at night, boy!" warned the old man in front of everybody as they rode away, "or he'll run off agin and jine his folks."

Annoyed, Dan plucked a sandburr off the top of his boot sock and felt his fingernails digging into his saddle blanket.

"I don't know why Uncle Buck keeps talking that way about him," Dan fretted to Monte who had heard the old man's remark. "I couldn't drive Chico off with a black snake."

"Maybe your great-uncle likes only mares," said the Indian lad, drily. "Maybe he's like the brown stallion."

After a full day's ride with Monte leading, they arrived at a water hole with grassy banks. How the Shoshone found it, Dan could not imagine. Beyond it, up the slope, lay a wilderness of cedar, juniper, and pine. In it, Dan knew, the wild ones were hiding with all the cunning of their breed.

The last part of their route was rough going. It led up the mountain through what Monte Wano called the down timber. Great pines and spruce, deadened by the fires of long ago, lay fallen in their path. The wind moaned weirdly through their splintered branches.

Once Freddie, usually well-behaved, became so frustrated at the difficult footing that he began bucking and running back down the mountain. That had only one result. Soon the duffle on his back was scattered over a hundred yards of landscape. Dan, on Chico, rode alongside and finally got him stopped.

For half an hour, the two boys backtracked the trail on foot, picking up food, blankets and cooking utensils. In spite of all the work, Dan could not help but chuckle at how funny the empty pack saddle looked hanging under Freddie's belly, all tangled up with his forelegs.

"He kicked our gear so high that the wild ones probably saw it sailing around in the sky and are now on their way to California," Dan said as he picked up a lost lash rope.

Two miles above the watering place, they selected a small ridge that commanded a view of the mountain slope for miles. Upon it, they dug a hole deep enough to conceal them and their bedding. Brush and dirt was used to roof it. A dead juniper was laid across its top to give it a natural look.

"This is a good hide-out if we stay down to do our

looking," said Monte Wano. "We'll probably have to spend two or three nights here. But I think we'll see them before they see us, or smell us."

Dan did something he had seldom done before. With his rope, he tied Chico to a cedar although permitting him a thirty-foot radius over which to graze.

"He follows me everywhere," Dan explained. "If I didn't tie him, he'd probably try to get in the dugout with us."

Monte Wano took a look above him at the outline of the tops of the mountain. "The snow patches are nearly all gone," he said. "I see only one or two. And they're pretty small. We'll soon find out what water hole they're using."

On the third morning, Monte was searching the slopes with the field glass. Dan was watching some ants carry small twigs across a rock at his feet. Suddenly Monte grew quiet and the glass didn't move.

He said, "I think they're coming." He handed the glass to Dan. "Take a look. Right up there above that bunch of green aspen." He pointed.

At first, Dan looked so hard that his eyes ached. But he didn't see anything moving. When he finally did see them, they looked no larger than the ants he'd been watching on the rock.

Quickly, the two boys rolled up their bedding. They slipped down behind the ledge where they'd left their horses. It was time to carry the word back to the Bar-B.

On their way back, they were careful to skirt the grassy-banked water hole so as not to leave their scent.

The Tailing

Four days later, around the grassy-banked water hole, the trap of canvas and bunting was laid. All was ready. The Shoshone scouts and the Bar-B hands were concealed in the surrounding foliage. Each man had with him his best mount.

Just as Pete Wano had said, it took only two hours once the water hole was located and the pack animals had delivered the materials.

Dan was opening and closing his mouth like a baby robin. He looked at the hidden ring of riders all around him. He knew they were excited because he was excited, too. He wondered how it would go this time. *We'll surely get back some of the steeldusts*, he thought. *But Jewel will be more difficult. She's smart and fast and tireless.*

Old Buck pulled his greatcoat closer about him. He snuggled down into his fur collar. Although there was a chill on the wind, the cloth corral and wing fence did not flap in the breeze. They were tightly stretched so they would not flutter and alarm the wild band.

Ben Dragoo was exploring the slope with his glass, Pete Wano at his side. The big mustanger had the keenest eyesight of anybody Dan had ever seen.

Pete Wano's idly roving gaze suddenly halted and

BEN and BUCK

sharpened. He pointed toward the misty top of Big Horn mountain.

"Mustangs," he said, softly, "they're a mile away and hundreds of feet above us. But they're comin' down."

Dan, behind him on Chico, stared and stared but saw nothing.

Again Pete Wano squinted into the hazy distance. His gaze steadied and his lips moved.

"They're pretty thirsty," he said. "They're walking with their heads down—just barely clearin' the grass."

Ben picked them up in his glass. "Yep!" he said, "there they are. They look like flies crawling down a wall."

"Do you see Jewel anywhere?" growled old Buck. "Do you see any of my mares?"

Ben said, "They're too far away, Mr. Boyce, for me to tell." He pushed the glass into the old man's hands. "Here, Mr. Boyce. Take a look."

"Naw!" muttered the old man. He pushed the glass away impatiently. "I can't see 'em. My eyes are gone. You tell me what you see, Ben."

Ben tried again with the glass but shook his head. "Now I've lost 'em," he said with disappointment, "but they're up there somewheres." Dan kept looking, but in vain.

Pete Wano shifted his position in his saddle with easy grace. He took another careful squint.

He grunted softly. "I think I see the little brown stud," he said. "He's the only one with his head up. He's prancing around like he owns the whole mountain. When he sees what we've got for him here, he'll be mad enough to eat the devil with his horns on."

Monte Wano moved his mount closer to Dan. "I've made up a poem about that brown stud," he said, keeping his voice low. "Do you want to hear it?"

Surprised, Dan nodded and wet his lips. He

hadn't known that his Shoshone friend wrote poetry. It seemed an odd time and place for a stanza of verse.

Then Monte began,

> *Four white feet*
> *And a white nose,*
> *Knock him in the head*
> *Feed him to the crows.*

A slow grin spread over Dan's face. "It's a good idea," he said, "only who's gonna do the knockin'?"

Finally Dan saw them. While some grazed here and there, it seemed to him that all were coming toward the water hole, making fewer and fewer stops for feeding. They all had their minds on the water.

"Let's all mount," Pete Wano passed the word along softly. There was the sound of rumps hitting saddles. "Stay on your horses. Don't move until we tell you. They're not as afraid of a man on a horse as they are of a man on the ground. A horse is a more familiar sight to them."

Now Pete's sharp eyes were identifying the different wild ones for Uncle Buck. "I see one, two, three gray ones, Mr. Boyce," he said. "They're probably your steeldusts. Wonder where the other two are? But I don't see the chestnut mare. Wait a minute! There she is—in the middle of the band. I'll bet she's still wearing the halter, too."

"Git her fer me, Pete, if you can," old Buck implored. "I'll probably never git this close to her agin."

Dan's eyes hurt from the strain of staring at the dark specks coming down off the mountain.

But Pete was still naming the mustangs, one by one.

"I see several new mares," he said, speaking low. "I see a sorrel. And a bay spotted with white. And a strawberry roan I don't recall seeing a year ago. That stud's sure got a lot of charm. I count twenty-five animals in all. One of them looks like a work mule off a farm."

Tex Tolbert laughed softly. "Yuh can't blame him fer joinin' the wild ones," he said. "He was gettin' tired pullin' that plow."

Two Shoshones, men of good judgment, had been sent around the mountain. They were the starters. It was their job to get behind the wild band and start them down the long slope

Dan's breathing came faster. He felt of the rope coiled on the right of his saddle horn. It was snug and tight. From the water hole, he could hear the small spring chattering over gravel. He felt sorry for the wild ones. Although they were very thirsty they would get no drink that day.

For another fifteen minutes the Bar-B party waited. Then Chico raised his head and looked in the direction of the mountain.

Pete Wano called out, "Get ready! They've started running."

They had indeed! The Shoshone starters, two small black objects, were riding down the mountains like demons. Ahead of them, raising a ribbon of dust, ran the wild ones. Every animal was in motion.

At the water hole, Chico chomped at the bit and pawed the ground nervously. Dan spoke to him quietly and reined him in. His own heart was hammering. What happened in the next few minutes was awfully important to the Bar-B.

Led by the brown stallion, the mustangs came bounding down the ridge like rolling boulders, their tails swishing and flaring out behind them like a luminous train behind a meteor. The mountain seemed alive with their motion.

They were coming exactly where Pete Wano wanted them to come. Their downhill pace was so pell-mell that Dan heard the crack of rocks and the snap of

101

brush as they rushed through it. Then they entered the area bounded by the bunting wing fences.

Dan forgot to look for the steeldusts. He had eyes only for Gaunch, the band's leader. The stud ran as if completely terrified. Dan could read it in his eyes, wide with panic. His nostrils were swelling red. Brown no longer, his body was dark with sweat.

He led the mares squarely between the aisle of cloth and bunting into the canvas corral. The Bar-B hands closed in behind them, preventing escape from that direction.

Round and round inside the small corral the mustangs milled, squealing with fear. Some went down. Others climbed upon the bodies of the fallen ones. But they did not try to smash through the canvas. Pete Wano had been right. Horses won't run into anything that looks solid. They won't try to jump something they can't see over.

And then one did see over it. The brown stallion, while climbing upon the bodies of the fallen mares, got a glimpse over the canvas at the outside world. In a flash, he leaped over it and sped through the brush to freedom. Eyes staring, Dan watched him go.

Another of the wild band, a chestnut mare with flowing mane and tail, saw his spectacular vault. Trodding on the same fallen bodies, she also cleared the canvas, her muscles quivering in the sunshine. Gathering herself and settling into a long stride, she followed the stallion. She still wore the halter.

Dan, on Chico, was posted on the outside of the corral, near the two escaping wild ones. Pete Wano on the coyote dun was near. So was old Buck, riding a black.

"That's Jewel!" shouted old Buck. "Don't let her git away, Pete!" His voice was hoarse and urgent.

Instantly Pete Wano, whirling his rawhide reata, swung the coyote dun into furious pursuit. But Dan

102

had moved even faster. The boy dug his heels into Chico's flanks.

"Go get her, Chico!" he yelled in the mustang's ear. He knew that he must overtake Jewel in the first three hundred yards, or not at all. Once she got in gear, calling upon all her Arab speed and stamina, she'd set the prairie on fire.

The grulla sprang forward so suddenly that Dan was jerked violently backward, and nearly fell out of the saddle. Recovering, he leaned forward, thrusting his boots deeply into the stirrups.

With both hands, he shook out the kinks in his rope, spreading it out behind and to the side, ready to toss. Never had he built a loop while traveling so fast. Chico was flying. The bite of the mountain air cooled Dan's face and made his eyes smart.

Now it was up to Chico. The grulla understood. It was his job to run down the mare, if he could. He knew that Dan wanted him to run her down. That was all the incentive he needed. His desire acted as an electric shock, rousing him to a super effort. The cacti and the sage rippled backward as his feet blurred over the plain.

The mare's rump came back to them, then her left flank, then her withers. Chico was running up her back.

It was then that Dan threw his rope—and missed! As it glanced off the mare's shoulder, his first feeling was one of heartsick despair. But he quickly forgot that when he saw that Chico, running as if a hundred devils were after him, still gained on the chestnut inch by inch.

Then a bold idea came to Dan, based on something that José had once shown him about bull-tailing, a pastime popular with the Mexican cowboys of Texas. Jewel's tail, long, reddish-brown and glossy, was flowing behind her like a pennant. Moving Chico closer, Dan seized the end of the mare's tail, wrapped

103

it securely around his wrist, and again around his saddle horn. Clutching it tightly, he pulled back on Chico's rein with his left hand.

Chico knew what that meant. In steer roping, it meant that the roper had tied onto the animal. Instantly, the grulla sat back, hind feet under him, fore feet thrust out in front, and received the shock.

For a moment the bodies of the two animals thrashed about. All forward motion stopped. Jewel stumbled and nearly went down. So did the lighter Chico. But sure-footed in the crisis, he stayed on his feet, binding her securely to him. And Dan clung like grim death to the end of the mare's tail, snubbed around his saddle horn.

Another rope sang freely past Dan's ear. It was a long throw, nearly thirty feet. It glided through the air like a tobacco ring blown halfway across the room by a pipe smoker. But its loop stayed flat and open. When it settled neatly around the struggling Jewel's neck, Dan knew that Pete Wano had thrown it.

Then the Shoshones and the cowboys moved in. After a short struggle, the mare was subdued. Quickly, she became her old, peaceful self.

Still mounted, Pete Wano walked his coyote dun around to the mare's side. Leaning over, he took his reata off her. He turned to Dan.

"That was the first time I ever saw a tailing on a horse, young man," he said, "You didn't leave me much to do."

Ben Dragoo rode up and dismounted. He approached Dan and Chico, admiration in his face.

"That was fast thinkin' and fast doin', Danny," the foreman praised. "I'm proud of you."

Chico was munching a tuft of bunch grass, moving forward a step at a time. Ben patted him on the rump.

"You're some hoss, Chico," he laughed. "You wasn't gonna let her git away, was you?"

Dan felt warm all over. But he was proudest of all for his horse.

Old Buck slid off the black. He advanced on the mare, his whiskery face strained with anger.

"You gol-derned she devil!" he scolded her. "Runned off from me, didn't cha! I oughta put a slug 'tween yore eyes and sell yer carcass fer glue!"

Recognizing him, Jewel nickered and thrust her nose into his open hand. And the old man melted completely.

A glad grin creased his leathery face. He passed an arm around her neck. Talking to her in low, tender tones, he began unbuckling the weathered halter she'd worn so long. She kept nuzzling in his hands and in his pockets.

"She's lookin' for raisins, Uncle Buck," laughed Dan. Seeing her up close for the first time, the boy was struck with her beauty.

"She'd probably like a drink, too," suggested Ben. But old Buck had already started leading her down to the green grass spring.

Back at the ranch, the old man led the chestnut into her old stall in the barn. For an hour, he brushed her and combed her. He talked to her in honeyed tones. She ate oats out of his hand. She nudged him with her nose. She had not forgotten the fare of other days nor the kindness of her old master.

Next morning, Ben came to Dan during breakfast. "Mr. Boyce wants to see you," he said, "at the big house. Soon as you get through eatin'."

With his mouth full of Carmen's scrambled eggs, Dan stared at the wall. *What's he going to chew me out about this time*, he wondered.

The old man was frank. "Set down, boy," he began, gruffly. Dan did.

"I bin tryin' to think of a way to thank you fer gittin' my mare back fer me when I bin kinda rough on you lately," the old man said.

Dan blinked and felt himself stiffening. He thought, *what do you mean by lately? You've been rough on me ever since I first walked through that door.* But he didn't say anything.

The old man went on, "I like the way you go after things. Yore gittin' bigger an' older. I bin thinkin' we otta send yuh to the high school at Elko. With Pete Wano's son. How'd you like thet?"

Dan sat still as stone, saying nothing. But he was thinking. He wants something from me, he told himself, or he'd never sweet talk me like this.

With a gnarled forefinger, old Buck tapped the tobacco down in his French brier pipe. "Ben thinks we oughta raise you to thirty-five a month," he went on. "Think yore worth it?"

"No," said Dan.

With a look of surprise, the old man plucked a match off his tobacco stand.

"Why not?" he asked.

"Because I don't rope well enough yet," said Dan. He blushed at having to admit it.

Old Buck scratched the match against the fireplace stones. Touching the flame to his pipe, he puffed slowly, keeping his eyes on Dan.

"All right," he said. "We'll leave you at twenty fer the present. Some day soon, I think we can do better than thet. Some day I think we can do better than thirty-five. I'm not gonna be here always. Some day, you might be runnin' the Bar-B."

Dan shifted his boots uncomfortably. What did he mean by that?

With the burnt-out match still in his hand, old Buck looked at the boy and laid it on the line.

"I want you to move up here to the big house and live with me," he said. "So's I can learn you about the

107

book work of runnin' a ranch. Tonia can cook fer us both."

Dan sat up sharply. He'd taken a whole lot off the old man just seeing him now and then. It would probably be much worse if he were living with him.

"Thank you, Uncle Buck," he said, his jaw firmly set. "But I believe I like the bunkhouse better." He didn't just believe he liked it better. He knew he did.

Surprise came again into the old man's face. "I know I bin kinda ornery to you, boy," he said, "but I'm not near as ornery as I act. I'd try to do better. I'd stay out of yore hair."

Dan shook his head. He looked his great-uncle right in the eye. "Nope," he said, "I think it's better if I don't."

The old man looked as if Dan had struck him. Defeat and disappointment lined his face. Worst of all, he looked lonely. Desperately lonely. In spite of himself, Dan felt sorry for him.

Old Buck laid his pipe on the smoking stand. For a moment he sat silent and brooding, twisting and folding his horny hands.

"It's funny," he said, "but lately I feel like the most important thing in the world fer me is to see my own kin folks oftener. An' yore the only one I got left."

Dan didn't say anything. He'd already said it.

"Well," the old man said, his voice almost hushed, "I guess that's that."

He took the pipe out of his mouth. He looked uncomfortable, as if he were about to say something that was hard for him to say. Then he said it.

"You shore gotta fine little hoss in that grulla. He's a Jim Dandy."

Dan's face lit up like the glow of a prairie fire. A warm grin grew on his lips. He felt proud—very proud—that his great-uncle had at last found one wild horse in Nevada that he respected.

Dan licked his lips and ran the whole thing over

in his mind. If the old man now liked Chico, they might get along better. Nearly all their disagreements had been over the mustang.

"Give me a little more time, Uncle Buck," he said. "I want to think some more on it."

Old Buck waved one hand. "Take all the time yuh want, boy," he said.

That night, Dan showed up at the big house carrying his worn bag, his rope, and his slicker. Tonia let him in. He could tell by the surprised look on her face that she didn't know what was going on.

Dan walked into the sitting room. Old Buck was seated at his desk.

"You still want me to stay with you up here?" Dan asked. Now that he was used to the old man's growling, he didn't think he'd mind it quite so much. Everybody was a little peculiar now and then.

Old Buck looked at him and nodded. "Shore do," he said.

Picking up his pipe, he lit it. He drew on it heavily. When he got it going good, he sent a single smoke ring twisting and curling and drifting halfway across the room. It reminded Dan of Pete Wano's lasso going thirty feet through the air to encircle Jewel's lovely neck.

Dan said, "If you'll just stop callin' me boy. That's what you called me the first day I got here. I never have got over it." He thought, *while we're talking we just as well get everything straightened out.*

Old Buck nodded. "All right, Dan," he said.

For a moment there was silence in the room. The only sound that could be heard was the lick of the flames in the fireplace.

Dan looked him straight in the eye. "Well," he said, "we might try it for a few days. If we don't get along I can always move back to the bunkhouse. But we could still be friends."

A glad look came into the old man's eyes. "Throw

109

yore gear right thar in thet south bedroom," he invited, pointing to its door. "It's all yores," he added. "Purty cool in thar. You can look out the west window into the pony pasture an' see yore hoss. Then come on in the dinin' room. Tonia's gittin' supper ready."